DEDICATION

To Laura—
For always saying what I need to hear

And Mom—
For never doubting

JOSH HOWARD

PERMUTED
PRESS

A PERMUTED PRESS BOOK
ISBN: 978-1-64293-863-0
ISBN (eBook): 978-1-64293-864-7

**PERMUTED
PRESS**

Permuted Press, LLC
New York • Nashville
permutedpress.com

Published in the United States of America
1 2 3 4 5 6 7 8 9 10

CHAPTER 1

As I watched the knife leave my stomach, blade shiny and slick with my own blood, I knew I was dead.

Thankfully, it was quick, nearly painless. But cold. The blade, I mean. Like a shard of ice through my gut. I never got a good look at my killer's face. Shadows danced and shifted, countering all my efforts to discover the person's identity. But there were others there too—formless shapes in the dark. Voices laughing. Screaming. Chanting.

"Soultorn."

"Bloodcursed."

"Shadespawn."

As the life left my body, I fell for what seemed like forever, through flames, then water. I sank into the blackest, deepest darkness, overwhelmed by the certainty that something worse was coming. "But I'm already dead," I thought. What could be worse than this?

That's when I woke up, sweating and gasping for breath. And then I got on my knees and prayed like I haven't prayed in a long time.

Not exactly the way I hoped to start my life at seventeen. Happy freakin' birthday to me.

So yesterday, Dad gave me this old journal. He said if I really want to be a writer, I needed to start writing.

Thoughts, ideas, experiences, it doesn't really matter as long as I write. Right now, my biggest claims to fame are the lyrics to all the songs I've written for Elijah's stupid band, including the ones about unrequited love and heartbreak that he's too dense to realize are actually all about him.

Anyway, this journal's a little worn and beat up, and the paper's yellowing at the edges. It's got character, as my dad would say. He said he picked it up at a garage sale and thought of me. I'm not exactly sure what to make of that.

He assures me that this isn't my only present. But I've got to wait until after our traditional birthday dinner to find out what else I'm getting. (Please, God, let it be something with four wheels.)

He wrote a little note on the inside front cover. It made me laugh.

"Hey, kid. The world is tough. It'll drag you down if you let it. Always remember who you are, where you came from, and that you're always loved. Do that, and nothing can stop you. Now get out there and kick some ass. Happy Birthday. Love, Dad."

Good old Dad. Simple and direct. He can be a little old-fashioned, so I do my best to humor him. Things always have to be done in a certain way in a certain order. He and Mom were pretty old when they adopted me. In their forties, I think. The birthday dinner became a tradition at some point. Just him, me, and Mom.

Mom. Next month marks two years she's been gone. I miss her like crazy.

But today's supposed to be a happy day, and I know that's how she would want it. So, I'm going to give it my best shot, creepy, unsettling nightmares be damned.

And...I smell bacon. Dad's actually cooking breakfast?! This I gotta see.

✓.☞▲.

Nara closed the red leather-bound journal and rolled out of bed. She slid thin, wiry legs into a pair of pajama pants, gathered her unruly mess of auburn hair into a loose knot, then crept down the stairs, anxious to catch a glimpse of this rare moment in Kilday family history. Were those pancakes she smelled too?!

She rounded the corner into the kitchen and stopped cold. Her dad was standing by the back door in full uniform, sheriff's badge nice and polished, a piece of bacon hanging from his mouth. A woman was handing him a sack lunch, a woman who didn't live there. Nara's dad hadn't made breakfast; this *woman* had. Just like that, Nara's appetite was gone.

Realization set in that the woman was Amanda Slater, the forty-something two-time-divorcee from church that Nara's dad had been spending a lot of time with. But never here, in their house. Nara's first thought was of her mother, but she pushed back against the sudden swell of emotions. She knew it was unfair to be upset with her dad—it had been two years, and he was lonely. But to see some other woman in her mom's kitchen, cooking with her mother's things, today of all days. How could he be so...thoughtless?

Suddenly aware of Nara's presence, they both turned and shouted, "Happy birthday!"

Nara forced a grin through gritted teeth. It took every ounce of strength to mutter the faintest and most tepid of thank yous.

"Amanda made us breakfast, but I gotta run, sweetie. Don't forget—big birthday dinner tonight!"

"Why the rush?" Nara asked, panicking. She couldn't believe he was really going to leave her alone with a virtual stranger.

"New lead in the Becca Howl case," he said, his face tightening. "Possible sighting out by Muddy Creek."

Becca had been missing for two weeks. Nara didn't really know her. They were the same age, but Becca was relatively new to town and a bit of an outcast. Her parents had a reputation for being junkies. Most people just assumed Becca ran off or was shacked up with some guy somewhere.

"Anyway, enjoy your breakfast. We'll talk tonight. Bye, ladies."

Nara attempted to mentally freeze her father in place, but it was no use. The door shut, and he was gone, leaving her alone. With Amanda.

An awkward moment of silence passed, and then they both spoke at once.

"I'm just gonna go get ready."

"Milk or orange juice?"

It was then that Nara saw it—the plate on the table with the number seventeen formed from pieces of bacon and the stack of pancakes impaled by seventeen tiny, multicolored candles. Great. She was going to have to sit there and have a conversation with this woman and eat her food.

Her dream had been right. There *was* something worse than death, and this was it.

CHAPTER 2

Showered, dressed, hair pulled back into a ponytail, Nara stepped outside. She was greeted by the autumn chill, an unpleasant reminder that she'd forgotten to grab her hoodie on the way out. But no way was she going back for it. The breakfast from hell had been torture enough. She'd also had to endure half an hour of Amanda insisting on packing her lunch and giving her a ride to school, the latter of which Nara flat out refused. She would rather freeze.

Halfway through the five-block trek, as she was starting to question the wisdom of that decision, Nara passed Mrs. Pulaski's house. Like every other morning, rain or shine, the eccentric old woman was outside pulling weeds and clipping bushes in her yellow robe and slippers. Today, however, she stopped and looked in Nara's direction.

"You see it?" she demanded.

Nara turned her head, making sure she was the only one around. "See what?"

Mrs. Pulaski raised her arm above her head, palm out. "Big one. Nine...ten feet. Scared the dickens out of Max and Bull. Kept 'em up barkin' all damn night."

Nara was completely lost. "I'm sorry, I don't—"

"One of *them*, from out in those damn woods. All gangly and hunched over, roaming up and down the street. And those eyes. I hope I never have to see those eyes again."

"Oh," Nara answered, forcing a smile, "Probably someone playing a prank. Halloween's in a couple weeks. You know how it is."

"I ain't stupid. I know what I saw."

Nara had just escaped one awkward conversation only to walk straight into another. "Well, have a nice day!" She abruptly turned and continued on her way.

Mrs. Pulaski raised her voice, repeating herself. "I ain't stupid! I know what I saw!"

Totally creeped out, Nara increased her pace. She couldn't wait to tell Hazy about this.

ᴧ☾☁

Nara crossed the threshold and into the halls of Darlington High, dodging and weaving through the swarms of cliques, circles, squads, packs, clubs, and other assemblages of peers that only served to aggravate her to the point of anxiety. She hadn't had a lot of success navigating the ever-changing demands of teenage social hierarchies. She'd always found herself hovering on the periphery, never quite finding the right fit anywhere. Never hot or cold, up or down, just existing somewhere in the middle. *Nara, the invisible girl*, as a former teacher had so rudely but accurately phrased it.

She stepped aside to narrowly avoid being crushed by a couple of roughhousing jocks. One of them pulled out a pencil and engaged in a mock-stabbing of the other. Her thoughts returned to her nightmare. The utter darkness. The vacant feeling of her own life slipping away. The weird voices.

"*Shadespawn.*"

She had tried to brush the whole thing off, but it nagged at her, stirring up feelings she didn't want to acknowledge...shadows of memories long buried.

Nara passed Jenny Mason's locker, which was being decked out with balloons, flowers, streamers, and string lights by her boyfriend, Mark. Jenny was the girl in Nara's class who happened to share the same birthday. Nara knew better than to expect a similar display of affection. Elijah could be sweet, but he wasn't exactly the most thoughtful guy. When it came to their on-again, off-again relationship, Nara had learned the hard way to set her expectations low.

Nara looked back. Jenny had just arrived, squealing in delight for all to hear, as if this kind of thing didn't happen to her every year. Momentarily distracted by the obnoxious display of emotion, Nara slammed into oncoming human traffic, getting a good douse of hot coffee. She slipped and fell backward, landing hard, sending one shoe airborne. Upon impact, the faulty zipper of her neon yellow backpack gave out, spewing forth books, papers, and a random assortment of lipstick, hair clips, and pads in every direction.

"What the hell, Nara?!"

It was Britney Kohl. Of course it was. Tall, fit, and gorgeous. And for reasons that Nara couldn't quite explain, her biggest nemesis since junior high. Out of four thousand potential students, Nara had to collide with her.

"I—I'm sorry, I—" Nara stammered.

"What is *wrong* with you? Look at my dress. It's *ruined*!"

Without hesitating, Britney poured her remaining coffee onto Nara's head. Britney's two sycophantic hangers-on, Violet Grey and Heather Lumis, laughed hysterically.

The altercation was already drawing a crowd. Nara scrambled, attempting to gather up her strewn books and personal items. She was soaked, embarrassed, and desperate to get away. At this moment, like so many moments before, she wished she truly were invisible.

Violet produced Nara's cast-off shoe. "Looking for this?" She pretended to offer it to her before launching it down the hallway. "Go get it!"

Nara choked back tears of rage and humiliation. No way would she let Britney and her parasites see her cry, but she felt too paralyzed to fight back. She hated that about herself.

Nara reached for the last of her belongings—the journal her father had given her, soaking in a puddle of coffee. Britney noticed the words *The Journal of Nara Kilday* scrawled on the front. She snorted. "You have *got* to be kidding me." She moved to grab it but was instead met by a firm shove, sending her stumbling backward.

"Leave her alone!" Hazy shouted.

Britney took a moment to compose herself. "Did you see what she did? My dress is *ruined*!"

"Back off before I smack those fake eyelashes off your face!" Hazy retorted, sticking her finger about an inch from Britney's nose.

A series of "Ooohs!" emanated from the crowd.

Britney looked past Hazy to Nara. "Be careful, Kilday. Next time your girlfriend may not be around to save you." Britney flipped her wavy strawberry blonde hair and strutted away. Violet and Julie followed, just as a janitor appeared from around the corner with a mop and bucket.

The crowd dispersed in disappointment. Hazy gave Nara a hand up and helped her finish gathering her things. "What a bitch."

Nara covered her face, fighting back tears. "I'm so embarrassed! I hate how she does that…how she makes me feel so…so helpless."

"It's because she always has an audience. She's only tough when she has a crowd to back her up. Look how fast she stood down when I gave it back to her."

"I know," Nara said, hands tightly gripping her journal. "I just—"

"Forget her. Let's get you cleaned up."

CHAPTER 3

In the bathroom, Nara finished washing the coffee out of her hair and changed into Hazy's DHS Volleyball sweatshirt. It didn't exactly smell fresh, but it was better than the alternative. At the sink, Hazy used a wad of paper towels to soak up the coffee from Nara's backpack.

Nara laid her journal out on the counter, assessing the damage. The back cover had absorbed most of the coffee, and a few pages were warped along the edges, but it was salvageable.

"You going to tell me what that's all about?" Hazy asked.

Nara looked into the mirror at Hazy. She never felt plainer and more uninteresting than when standing next to her best friend. She was naturally beautiful, but the way her sleek black hair contrasted her pale skin and bright red lips only made her more striking. Still, Hazy was not your typical beauty. She stood out from the crowd, and it wasn't just her trademark style or headband she wore almost daily. She had an edge to her, an aura of depth that let you know she wasn't to be mistaken for a member of any shallow social clique.

"It was a present from my dad. He wants to encourage my writing," Nara answered, eyes downcast.

Hazy grabbed another handful of paper towels. "That's nice. Though I know you were hoping for something a little more…drivable."

"True, but the only extra car in the driveway this morning was Amanda Slater's," Nara said, making no effort to hide her contempt.

Hazy's eyes went wide. "*What*?! I didn't know it was that serious!"

"Yeah, well, I didn't either. Or…I was hoping it wasn't. But I went downstairs this morning, and she was in our kitchen cooking breakfast."

"Go, Sheriff Kilday!" Hazy said, laughing.

Nara cringed. "Gross. Please don't ever do that again."

"Whatever. Your dad's human too. Heard anything from Elijah yet?" Hazy asked.

"No, but I've been dropping hints like crazy all week that I want him to take me to see that screening of *Beetlejuice* at the Limelight. He knows how much I love that movie."

Hazy raised an eyebrow. "When you say *hints*…"

"I sent him a selfie of me in front of the marquee with a text that said, 'Let's do this for my birthday' and a link to buy the tickets."

Hazy grimaced and then shook her head. "Okay, well, if that doesn't do it then you should definitely dump him. For good this time."

"I don't know how much fuel is left in that tank anyway. Feels like we've been running on fumes lately."

"*Lately*? You mean for the past six months? I know you care about him, but face it. It's over. You deserve better."

"It's not like I have guys lining up to go out with me."

"You sell yourself too short. Have some confidence. Guys like that."

Nara rolled her eyes. "I guess. So, are you going to tell me what's going on with you?"

"What do you mean?"

"Come on. I've known you forever. There was a little something extra to that push you gave Britney."

Hazy continued to absentmindedly scrub at the stains on Nara's backpack. "Mom left her phone out. Dad went snooping. Sounds like she's cheating again."

"Oh, no."

"Yeah. It's bad. If she leaves, I don't know what me and Simon are going to do. Dad's totally dependent on her. His health just gets worse all the time. How the hell are we going to take care of him and pay the bills? I freaking hate her."

Nara took her by the hand. "I'm sorry. Want me to have my dad arrest her?"

"Ha! It's probably only a matter of time anyway. I think she's using again."

Nara hesitated. Despite their years of friendship, she always felt a little awkward when broaching topics of a spiritual nature. "I know it sounds corny, but for what it's worth, I'll be praying for you guys."

"Coming from you, it means everything."

"I guess we should be getting to class."

"Oh, wait! I almost forgot. Here," Hazy said, pulling a small box wrapped in red paper from her purse. "Happy birthday."

"Hazy! I told you not to get me anything. You've got enough to worry about."

"Oh, please. Just open it."

Nara tore away the red paper and opened the box. Inside was a silver necklace with a star-shaped pendant.

"It's really nice, but umm...."

"Don't freak out," Hazy said, rolling her eyes. "I know what you're thinking. But the pentacle, right side up, has historically been a symbol for good. The five points are supposed to represent different virtues or positive traits or something. All good things! It's only when it's turned upside down that it starts to get all Satan-y."

"Wow, okay. I love it. It's beautiful...just a little... unexpected."

"A cross would have been too on the nose, and a heart just isn't my style. Think of it as a symbol of our friendship. Or give it your own meaning, I don't care. I just want you to look at it and remember how strong and brave you really are. And to know you're never alone. Even when Britney is being a total bitch."

"I don't know what to say. I don't think of myself as either of those things. Far from it, actually."

"And that's why I love you. Now turn around." Hazy placed the necklace around Nara's neck, connecting the clasp in the back. "There, perfect."

Nara nodded and smiled, then looked down at the necklace. She had to admit, despite whatever implications it had, it *was* beautiful.

CHAPTER 4

After homeroom, Nara found her locker in the same state she'd left it in yesterday—no balloons, no streamers, not even a card. Annoyed at the twinge of disappointment she felt, she exchanged her algebra textbook for her American history spiral and mussed her stringy, wet hair in the mirror affixed to the inside of her locker door. A familiar face appeared over her shoulder in the reflection, brandishing that cocky grin and those big blue eyes that had always been her weakness.

She turned around and Elijah threw his arms around her, lifting her off the ground in a suffocating hug. "Happy birthday to my favorite girl!"

"Um, are you okay?" Nara asked, startled by Elijah's unusually demonstrative behavior.

"Are *you* okay?" He set her down and looked her over. "I heard about earlier."

Nara shut her locker door. "Yeah, I'm fine. So, listen. I have to have dinner with my dad tonight, but we should be done by seven. That should give us plenty of time to get to the Limelight by eight."

Elijah hesitated. "Uh…yeah. About that. Me and the guys got booked for a gig tonight in Barksdale."

"Very funny. But seriously, I'll text you when we're done, and you can just pick me up from the restaurant."

"No, babe. I'm for real. We're opening for the Scum Rats. We couldn't exactly pass it up. It could be huge opportunity for us. You understand, right?"

Any remaining sliver of hope Nara had about salvaging her birthday collapsed into a dumpster fire of disappointment. She responded through gritted teeth and a sarcastic smile. "Of course. Spending an evening with your girlfriend on her birthday...or the Scum Rats. Oh, I completely understand."

"Exactly! I see you all the time. And it's an old movie we can watch at home whenever anyway. I told the guys you'd be cool about it." He moved in to hug her again. "You're the best."

Nara recoiled. "Don't. Just...don't." She turned and quickly escaped into the chaotic, flowing throngs of teenagers.

"Nara!" Elijah called after her. "We still good?"

Students of Mr. Dargo's American History class filed on to stark yellow school buses, embarking on the annual field trip to Veilwood Forest. Nara wasn't particularly thrilled at the idea of a half-hour hike into the woods to look at some old rocks, but considering how the rest of her day had gone, she was coming around to the idea. At least she could avoid Elijah for a couple of hours.

Waiting in line to board, she noticed a familiar face standing to the right side of the bus doors, appearing to cross off names on a list. When the tall, dark-haired boy with glasses made eye contact with Nara, his passive, sullen face lit up.

"Simon!" Nara almost shouted, grinning wide. "What are you doing here?"

Simon's face went red. "Oh, hey, Nara. I'm just, you know, helping out Mister Dargo on the trip. Teacher's aide and all. How've you been? Haven't seen you over in a while. Then again, I don't see Hazy that much anymore either. Have you ever been out to the site? It's amazing."

"Nope."

A long moment stretched on while the two stared at each other, both seemingly waiting for the other to elaborate. Someone behind Nara coughed.

"Oh," she said, snapping out of it, "I'm sorry, I'm probably screwing up your headcount or whatever. I'm sure I'll see you out there, or whatever."

"Yeah, cool."

Nara turned to step onto the bus, but Simon's voice stopped her. "Um…Happy Birthday, Nara."

Nara stopped dead in her tracks and felt her face go hot. "Thank you," she said sheepishly. She had known Simon to be many things but never sweet or thoughtful.

Nara climbed into the bus and took a seat near the back and waited. Moments later, Hazy rushed on board to join her. "Where have you been?" Nara asked.

"Sorry. I was talking to Mike," Hazy said, flipping open her compact to reapply her lipstick.

"Talking, huh?"

Hazy ran her fingers through her hair and adjusted her headband. "There was *some* talking."

"Seriously?" Nara said, incredulous. "What about Kyle?"

"He never texted me back."

"It's been two days!"

"Well, you snooze, you lose."

Nara slapped her forehead in frustration. "Ugh! You drive me so crazy sometimes! Speaking of which, your brother wished me happy birthday. Did you put him up to that?"

"Simon wished you happy birthday? Is he sick? He hasn't remembered my birthday in years. But no, it wasn't me. Guess I shouldn't be surprised, though."

"What do you mean?"

"Nothing. Never mind," Hazy said, avoiding eye contact with Nara.

"No, you can't do that. What did you mean?"

Hazy let out a deep breath. "Are you telling me you had no idea?"

"No idea about what?"

"I can't believe we're having this conversation. Listen to me—this doesn't leave this bus. It doesn't even leave this seat, understand? Simon…God, I feel gross saying this out loud…Simon has a thing for you. Or *had* a thing for you."

"What do you mean *a thing*?"

"Why do you think everything changed and he stopped hanging around us? He got drunk and let it slip to me once. I told him to stay away, or I'd kill him. I wasn't about to let him do something stupid to hurt our friendship. But you can't tell him I told you!"

Nara sat back in shock. "I won't. I just can't believe you never told me."

"I'm sorry, I was just trying to keep things from getting weird."

At that moment, Simon came aboard. He looked toward the back of the bus and grinned at Nara before sitting down next to Mr. Dargo.

"Well," Nara said, shrinking down in her seat, "things just got weird."

CHAPTER 5

One hour, several bug bites, and two scraped knees later, Nara, along with eighty of her classmates, stood deep within Veilwood Forest on the roughly fifty acres of land from which the town of Darlington Hills got its name.

Despite her frustration with the way her birthday was playing out, she had to admit that the forest was much more impressive than she had ever imagined.

Winding through the trees were long, continuous rows of tall, earthen mounds, as well as several larger freestanding conical structures. But Nara was most impressed by the dilapidated remnants of numerous stone monuments and enormous half-buried pyramid shapes covered in soil, moss, and vines. It was like she had stepped into another world.

Mr. Dargo climbed to the top of a massive, cracked stone pedestal and struck a pose. Nara had recognized early on that he had a certain flair for the dramatic. His stern features, deep-set eyes, and perfectly styled hair just added to his aura of a man who took himself way too seriously. He cracked open his history text and began to read.

"In 1836, while searching for his young daughter who had wandered off his homestead into the woods, pioneer William Darlington discovered a series of unusual mounds and small hills."

Almost instantly everyone's attention was diverted to a group of tightly huddled jocks making obscene gestures. Dargo paused to deliver an icy glare in their direction. One thing you learned almost right away in Mr. Dargo's class—he did not suffer fools.

He cleared his throat and continued. "Upon closer inspection, he realized that these hills weren't natural, but were actually man-made stone structures and burial mounds that had, over time, been reclaimed by the forest. William Darlington became convinced that he had found evidence of some long-lost civilization and began writing to all the newspapers of the day, proclaiming his discovery, soon dubbed the Darlington Hills. The name became shorthand for the entire area as more settlers arrived over the next ten years.

"Sadly, during that time, Darlington's wife and two sons passed from sudden illness. Eventually, Darlington himself succumbed to alcoholism and died alone and penniless, never truly appreciated by historians of the day for his magnificent discovery. Some claimed that he and his family had fallen under a curse for disturbing the ancient site. Whether true or not, it was enough to keep people away. Knowledge of the ruins fell into myth and legend."

Mr. Dargo closed the book and appeared to stare wistfully into the forest. "It wasn't until the middle of the last century that interest resurged, and researchers officially designated the site as Native American in origin—not evidence of some lost civilization as William Darlington believed. However!" Mr. Dargo exclaimed, raising a finger, "Many dispute those findings and still subscribe to Darlington's theories."

A single hand shot into the air.

"Yes, Britney?"

"What about the little girl? Whatever happened to her?" she asked. A smattering of laughter broke out among the students.

"Great question, Britney. The story is so incredible that few remember the young girl's part in it. Very perceptive of you."

Nara and Hazy exchanged looks, rolling their eyes.

"Unfortunately, William Darlington never found his daughter Sara. Her fate remains a mystery."

Duane Rodd, huge arms bursting out of his football jersey, blurted, "Do we get extra credit if we find her bones?" The query was met with a series of groans and chuckles.

Mr. Dargo smirked. "You think that's funny, Mister Rodd? Ten points off your final grade. How's that for a laugh?"

Duane shirked back into the pack of jocks.

"Now, everyone is free to explore the site for the next hour. This assignment counts as fifty percent of your final grade this semester. So take pictures, notes, sketches, rubbings—just please try not to disturb anything. These ruins have stood for centuries, and we want to preserve them, right? Now get to it!"

The students dispersed, breaking off into small groups. Hazy turned to Nara. "So, where do you want to start?"

As Nara opened her mouth to answer, Simon appeared next to them. "I've got the perfect spot. Follow me." He stepped off the main trail and slid down a short incline that led deeper into the forest.

Nara turned to Hazy. "Well?" she said quietly. "Are you coming, or would you prefer I go off with him alone?"

Hazy closed her eyes and groaned.

Nara laughed. "That's what you get for the comment about my dad earlier."

Simon turned back towards the girls. "It's totally safe, I promise! I've been down this way half a dozen times. The ruins extend another hundred yards in this direction. This is where the best stuff is, trust me."

Hazy extended her arm, brandishing a sarcastic smile. "After you, birthday girl."

They followed Simon's lead, carefully stepping over fallen branches and castoff stones. The trees became closer and more abundant the farther they ventured. As the noise of eighty of their fellow teenagers began to fade, the crunching of their footsteps over dead leaves grew louder in the deep quiet of the forest.

After several minutes, Nara and Hazy had almost completely lost sight of Simon when they heard him call out, "Over here!"

The girls pressed on through the thick tangle until it abruptly ended at an open clearing. Within, arranged in a circle, was a series of massive, upright stones emerging like teeth from the forest floor. Simon stood near the center, arms outstretched. "Welcome to Darlington Hills' own Stonehenge!"

Hazy spun around, taking it all in. "Whoa. This is seriously wicked. I can't believe you never told me about any of this!"

"I've tried. Several times. You just don't listen."

Nara remained at the edge of the circle, apprehensive. Whatever this place was, she didn't like it. Like the children's puzzles that ask you to find the thing that doesn't belong, that was this place. Something about it was just…wrong.

"What's this all of this supposed to be? What's it doing here?" Hazy asked.

"No one really knows. Unlike the rest of the ruins, this spot wasn't discovered until the last couple of decades. The theory is that this is where they—whoever they were—performed their rituals." Simon ran his hand over a smooth, elevated slab at the center. "This was likely an altar for prayer or meditation."

Hazy dramatically slung her body across the stone. "Or sacrifices!"

"Historically, sacrificial victims were selected for their purity. That definitely rules you out."

Hazy rose up and punched him in the shoulder. "Jerk!"

Nara took a hesitant step into the circle, the drumming of her own heartbeat drowning out Hazy and Simon's bickering. She slowly made her way around the perimeter, studying the towering stones that stood nearly twice her height. Etched onto their surfaces were vertical patterns of strange hieroglyphs. Nara stopped cold in her tracks. Something clawed at the recesses of her mind, like a forgotten melody trying desperately to reassert itself.

"What are these?" she asked, the words feeling slow and thick in her mouth.

"Most likely a forgotten language," Simon answered. "Although there's too many pieces missing, so no one's been able to make much sense of it. What little research that's been done is conflicting."

"Nara?" Hazy said, stepping closer to her best friend. "Are you okay?"

Hazy's voice was just a distant muffle as all of Nara's focus was drawn to the ancient writing. As if someone else was in control of her body, she reached out and touched the stone.

Then everything went black.

Nara was no longer in the forest but back in her dream, watching it all play out again. The knife, the fall, the voices.

"*Shadespawn.*"

Then she saw them—the symbols. They had always been there, hovering just on the edge of her memory. But now, they burned like a fire in her mind. And in the darkness, another presence made itself known. It began as the faint sound of a crying child then morphed into the piercing shriek and fury of something hideous. Something watching her.

Nara tried to scream but there was no breath left in her body. She fell.

CHAPTER 6

A murky blur of green and grey slowly coalesced into the image of swaying treetops and an overcast sky. At the edges of Nara's vision, something else came into focus—the gawking faces of dozens of her classmates.

Nara's face went hot as she realized that she was sprawled out on the ground, flat on her back. She had no memory of how she got there.

A muffled, repetitive sound in her ears resolved into the distinct voice of Mr. Dargo.

"…Okay? Nara! Nara, can you hear me?" His face entered her field of vision, as did those of Hazy and Simon, who were crouching down in the grass beside her. Hazy was squeezing the life out of Nara's left hand.

"What happened?" Nara asked, the words coming out dry and cracked.

Mr. Dargo placed his cold hand across her forehead. "Just stay still. The paramedics are on their way."

Words spilled out of Hazy's mouth in a rush. "Are you okay? I kept calling to you, but you acted like you didn't even hear me. One minute you were just standing there then the next you just collapsed."

Before Nara could respond, she heard snickering coming from somewhere among the onlookers. It only took her a moment to zero in on the culprit. Britney locked eyes with her, making no effort to hide her amusement. She turned to whisper something to Violet and they both erupted with laughter.

Nara sat up, keeping her eyes on Britney. "I'm fine."

Mr. Dargo placed his hands on her shoulder. "You should stay put until the paramedics arrive. You may have injuries—"

"I said I'm fine," Nara interrupted.

Hazy helped brush the leaves from Nara's hair and backside. "You sure you're okay?" she asked.

"I just want everyone to stop looking at me," Nara responded through gritted teeth.

Hazy nodded, her eyes narrowing. She quickly stood up and turned to the crowd. "Okay, that's enough!" she yelled, "Give the girl some space for God's sake."

Nara felt a gentle nudge and turned around. Simon was offering a bottle of water from his backpack. Nara may have been the one to pass out, but Simon looked pale enough to fall over dead. Was he worried about her?

"Here you go," he said.

Hazy stuck her finger in his chest. "You too. Just back off a minute."

"No, it's okay. He's fine. Thank you, Simon." Nara took the water, wondering again at Hazy's revelation about her brother. Did he still harbor feelings for her? Or was she just reading too much into simple gestures of kindness?

"Over here!" Mr. Dargo shouted, jumping up and down waving his arms.

"Just stay put," he said, turning to her. "The paramedics are here and will get you all checked out."

Nara rolled her eyes. "Great."

Two hours and one stern admonishment to "get plenty of rest and fluids" later, Nara was on her way home, riding shotgun in her father's police cruiser. She felt good enough to finish the school day, but once Sheriff Kilday got the call, the decision was made for her.

"Are you sure you don't want me to call Doctor Walsh? I know he'd fit you in today."

"Dad, I'm fine. I promise. I think I just got too hot out there. I didn't have anything to drink all day."

"Too hot? It's fifty degrees out."

"Yeah, but there was a lot of hiking. I worked up a pretty good sweat. You ever been out there? To the ruins?"

Her dad didn't answer immediately. For a moment, Nara wondered if he had even heard her.

"Yeah, sure," he finally said. "Once. A long time ago."

"And?"

"Wasn't that impressed. You sure you're okay?" he asked, steering the conversation back to Nara. "Would you like me to have Amanda come over and stay with you until I get home?"

"No!" Nara shouted, and then caught herself. "I mean, I'm just going to lay down. You don't need to bother her."

"Thing is…something has come up. I'm going to be working late tonight. We're going to have to postpone your birthday dinner. I'm sorry."

"Oh," Nara said, desperately trying to hide her disappointment. "Well, I understand."

"I'm really sorry, sweetie. It's just…it looks like we may have another missing girl."

"What? Who?"

"Melani Reilly. Hasn't been seen in three or four days. Had a big fight with her parents and ran off. They assumed she was staying with a friend. But none of her friends have seen her. Have you heard anything by any chance?"

Melani Reilly. Another girl Nara's age. "No, but I don't really know her. We run in different circles." Who was she kidding? Nara didn't even have a circle. Regardless, Melani was one of the more likable girls in Nara's class. She couldn't be more different than Becca Howl. "Do you think there's a connection?"

"I…I have no idea. Right now, I just need you at home safe, for my own peace of mind. And if you had any other birthday plans…maybe postpone those too."

Too late, she thought. Elijah already took care of that.

"In fact, maybe I'll send Amanda over so you're not alone. Maybe you two can get to know each other a little better."

Nara cringed. How could she steer this in another direction without hurting her dad's feelings?

"Can we compromise? Can I just have Hazy over? I'll stay home, you won't have to bother Amanda, and my birthday won't be a total bust."

Her father kept his eyes glued to the road, but his thoughts seemed a million miles away.

Finally, he said, "Okay. That's fair. But you have to promise me that you'll stay home. And keep all the doors locked. Understood?"

"Yeah, Dad. I get it," she said, perhaps a bit too flippantly.

"Nara…."

Nara let out a long sigh, looking out the window and rolling her eyes.

"I promise, Dad, okay? I promise."

Nara wiped the steam-fogged mirror. For a moment, she felt as if she was looking into a stranger's eyes. The silver pentacle around her neck, cold against her naked skin, only added to the sense of visual dissonance. The hot shower may have washed away the day's filthy accumulation of coffee, sweat, dirt, and humiliation, but it did nothing to rid Nara of the creeping dread at the back of her mind. But she knew the true source of her unease had nothing to do with the necklace, or even Elijah, Britney, or the missing girls. After what had happened in the woods, she couldn't help wondering if her dream wasn't a dream at all—but a warning.

Nara pulled her damp hair into a ponytail, dressed in comfortable shorts and a t-shirt, then checked her phone. A couple of missed calls from Elijah and a text from Hazy. Elijah could sweat it out. Was it hoping for too much that he'd be so consumed with guilt that his show would bomb? Probably. She opened Hazy's text.

Sorry. Can't hang tonight. Shit to deal with. Mom & Dad had a huge fight. Call u later.

And there it was. The perfect end to a terrible day. She'd be spending the evening of her birthday alone. She was crushed, but reminded herself it was unfair to blame

Hazy. Her parents had been caught in this cycle for what seemed like forever, and they never spared neither her nor Simon any of its ugliness. If nothing else, it helped put things in perspective. Nara might not ever feel her mother's embrace again, but she would always have the cherished memories of their time together. Hazy had known nothing but pain and disappointment most of her life.

Nara typed her response and hit send.

So sorry. Whatever you need, I'm here for you.

All she could do now was make the best of her situation. After her train wreck of a day, maybe an evening to herself was exactly what she needed.

Doors locked, curtains drawn, lights turned down, she stopped by the kitchen, popped a bag of popcorn, grabbed *Beetlejuice* from the DVD shelf, then sprinted back upstairs to her bedroom. As she queued up the movie and turned her phone to silent, she realized she didn't need Elijah and an audience full of obnoxious hipsters. This was *her* night, and she was going to enjoy it.

That's the moment her foot caught in the strap of her backpack, which she had carelessly left lying on the floor. A shower of books, pencils, and popcorn exploded into the air as Nara tripped and went tumbling headfirst into her nightstand. She rolled over and away from the chaos, wincing in pain and indignity. Blood ran down her forearm from where she had raised her hand to shield the blow to her face.

She picked herself up and hobbled to the bathroom where she did a full assessment of the damage. Aside from the cut to the palm her right hand, a scraped knee a scratch to the forehead seemed to be the worst of it. After cleaning up the blood and applying a Band-aid to the wound, she returned to her bedroom. After one look at the mess she had made, Nara decided that was it. *I'm done.*

There was to be no salvaging her seventeenth birthday.

She couldn't even be bothered to care as she stepped through popcorn and kicked past crumpled textbooks on the defeated march to her bed. The only thing that gave her pause was that God-forsaken red journal, lying open on the floor to two blank pages. The stupid thing practically stared back at her, taunting her to unburden herself of an entire day's worth of misery onto its empty pages.

Instead, she kicked it aside, climbed into bed, and pulled the covers up over her head. Her last thought was of Simon as she surrendered herself to sleep's blissful escape.

CHAPTER 7

Her phone's alarm harshly announced the arrival of 6 a.m. Nara cracked one eye open and cursed the world. She forced a hand out from her warm blanket-cocoon, fumbling blindly to silence the jarring intrusion, and was instantly rewarded with a painful reminder of last night's ungraceful episode. Her palm was sore and sticky. When she pulled her hand back under the blanket, she realized the Band-aid had come off during the night, leaving her hand covered in blood. Perfect.

Nara checked her missed messages, squinting from the blinding brightness of her screen. Nothing from Hazy. Nothing from Elijah. She had expected at least one late night groveling text from him. Just two texts from Dad. One letting her know he was sorry and would likely be working through the night, and another asking her to check in with him when she woke up. She sent off a quick *All good. Love you,* and then to Hazy, *Just checking on you. Hope you're okay.*

As Nara pulled back the covers from over her head, vision adjusting in the dim light, she received her second alarm of the morning. There was blood everywhere—covering her blankets, pillows, and t-shirt, even splotched all over her arms. It was like a crime scene. She threw back the covers and dashed down the hall in a panic, running to the bathroom and furiously scrubbing her hands under scalding water. As the blood washed away, she examined the wound on her palm again. Was it her imagination or did it appear wider and deeper than it had been last night? A simple Band-aid clearly wasn't up to the job. She found a little bit of left-over gauze from her dad's knee surgery and wrapped it up tight. She knew once he saw it, he was going to freak out and insist she get it looked at.

Nara returned to her bedroom and flipped on the light. On top of the bloody mess that she'd made in her bed, books, papers, and popcorn still lay strewn about. Whatever curse her seventeenth birthday unleashed had carried over to today. She was relieved that at least Dad hadn't come home late in the night to the chaos, and she certainly didn't want him to discover it while she was at school. With only a few minutes to spare before she needed to get ready, she started stripping the bed and pillowcases. When she tugged at her bedspread, something shook loose and plunked onto the floor at her feet.

Her eyes widened. It was her journal. She was certain had left it out laying in the floor last night—so how had it gotten into her bed and lost within in the tangle of her blankets? She picked it up and noticed dry splotches of blood visible even against the bright red cover. Nara opened it to the first page to find yesterday's entry smeared in red slashes, followed by page after page of filled with markings of the same deep crimson—not random or haphazard, but crudely defined shapes and patterns. Their resemblance to the stone hieroglyphs in the woods was unmistakable. Nara gasped and dropped the journal like it was on fire.

The horror of what had happened began to dawn on her. She put her head in her hands and dropped to her knees. "No. No. No. No. No." A nightmarish vision played out in her mind—waking up in the night, captive to some unseen force, drawing from her own wound to transcribe the strange runes in blood. Ice cold fear shot through her veins, summoning the specter of buried memories. It was happening again. The thing she dreaded most, the dark cloud from her past that she blamed for creating the invisible gulf between herself and everyone else. There were questions she never had answers for, thoughts and feelings she had only managed to keep at bay through persistent faith and belief.

She clung to those things, but for the first time wondered if they would truly be enough.

CHAPTER 8

Nara made it to homeroom with only seconds to spare—not that it mattered. Students and teachers milled about, hugging, crying, consoling each other. No one had seemed to take Becca Howl's disappearance too seriously. But Melani Reilly was a different story. Cheer squad, student council, tennis star—the girl was popular and beloved.

Rumors and gossip passed like currency. The girls had met some older man online. They had run off to Florida to star in adult movies. They had been kidnapped by a drug cartel. No story was too far-fetched or salacious, as long as it allowed people to avoid confronting what they all feared the most—that the girls were dead and there was a killer living among them.

Students who normally never had anything to say to Nara were striking up awkward conversations. She knew what they were after, though. As the daughter of the sheriff, they were digging for any juicy scraps of inside information. Even if she had been privy to any confidential info from her father, these people would be the last ones she would share it with. Considering her lack of any kind of social standing, chances were they all knew more about what was going on than she did anyway.

After first period, Nara waited for Hazy at the usual spot next to the water fountain by the southside stairwell. She was eager to find out how things had gone yesterday, hoping against hope for good news. She hadn't decided if she was going to let Hazy in on her own crises just yet. What could she say that wouldn't make her sound like a total lunatic? She unconsciously fidgeted with her necklace, running her fingers across the edges of the five-pointed star.

A minute and a half passed and there was still no sign of Hazy. Instead, Nara was greeted by the last person she wanted to see today, other than Elijah.

"You look like Hell, Kilday," Britney said. Violet, her less attractive shadow, snorted. Nara had always been baffled by Violet's acceptance among the in-crowd. Her midnight black hair, pale skin, and style of dress screamed "slutty goth Halloween costume" more than "preppy pride of Darlington High."

Britney tucked a lock of strawberry blonde hair behind her ear and bent over for a drink from the fountain. Nara couldn't help but notice the gawking looks from passing boys as Britney's backside peeked out from beneath her too-short skirt. Nara hated how self-conscious it made her feel—how she *always* felt in Britney's presence.

"You hear the news?"

"My dad *is* a cop."

Britney seemed bristle at her response. She wiped her mouth. "I wasn't talking about Melani, dumbass. You missed a great show last night."

Nara's felt her stomach turn. Was she talking about Elijah? Had she actually gone to his show or was she just trying to get under her skin?

"You have terrible taste in music. They suck," Nara said bluntly. She anxiously scanned the hallway for Hazy. Where was she?

Violet laughed. "Oh, there was some sucking all right!"

Violet wasn't just taunting her. Something had happened. Nara felt sick.

As if on cue, her backpack buzzed. Her hand shook as she pulled back the zipper and reached inside to retrieve her phone. She was expecting Hazy or her dad, but instead found a text notification from an unknown number. As she swiped to open her messages, she became vaguely aware of some commotion around her—people stopping, laughing, and pointing.

The message opened. It was a single image, somewhere outside, behind a bar or a club. People could be seen standing around talking and smoking, but there was no mistaking the central focus—two people locked in a passionate kiss, hands groping, blissfully ignorant of anything or anyone else around them.

Elijah.

And Hazy.

Nara looked up to see dozens of students looking down at their phones, sharing them with friends—some aghast, some in sheer delight. The photo had practically gone viral. Nara felt the room spin. She wanted to run and hide, wanted to scream, but her legs and her willpower had turned to rubber.

Britney hovered somewhere in her peripheral vision, cackling with perverse satisfaction. There was a sudden hush among the crowd as they parted like the Red Sea.

There she was. Nara didn't know what she had expected—that her best friend would have grown horns and a tail? That she'd be brandishing a wicked smile, gloating in triumph? It would have made hating her a lot easier. Instead, the Hazy standing before appeared broken and ashamed, her face red with tears. Somehow, it only made Nara angrier. She had been betrayed in the worst way possible, and she wasn't about to let Hazy rob her of her outrage.

Her mind scrambled, trying to assemble the right combination of words. She envisioned herself launching into a tirade of righteous indignation. The words "You're just like your mother" danced at the tip of her tongue. Twenty-four hours' worth of pent-up frustration added extra fuel to her fire. She was ready to explode. She gathered her courage, balled her fists, walked right up to Hazy…

…and kept on walking.

CHAPTER 9

Nara sat outside on the cold concrete steps of the south side exit and cried.

Her favorite red hoodie was meager protection against the frigid autumn wind, but she didn't care. She had the fire of anger to keep her warm. Anger at Hazy and Elijah. Anger at Britney. Anger at herself.

Once again, she had backed down, tucked tail, and ran. In past confrontations, she had held strong to the belief that she was taking the moral high road by walking away and turning the other cheek. But she'd been fooling herself. It was all a lie. It wasn't morality that drove her to avoid conflict. She was just a gutless coward, plain and simple.

She felt trapped. She didn't have the strength to endure another day of stares, gossip, and God knows what else. She just wanted to escape. If only she could just lie down, close her eyes, and never wake up. If only she could be with Mom again….

A familiar voice shook Nara from her dark reverie.

"Mind if I join you?"

Nara quickly wiped the tears from her face. "Did *she* send you?"

Simon sat down on the steps next to Nara. "Nope. She won't even talk to me. Here," he said, removing his jacket. "You look like you're freezing."

"I'm fine."

Simon placed his jacket around her shoulders anyway.

"I said I'm fine."

For a few moments, they sat in silence, both looking anywhere and everywhere but at each other.

Nara grabbed the edges of his jacket and pulled it tight around her arms. "Thank you," she said.

"You're welcome."

"So, you heard?"

"I think most of the school has."

Nara buried her head in her hands.

"I'm sorry. That came out wrong. Do you want me to go?"

Nara lifted her head. "Just say what you came here to say."

"I'm sorry for what happened. I'm not going to apologize for my sister. She's always been a little…reckless. But I know she really cares about you. Whatever happened last night, I don't believe it was intentional."

"So, she accidentally fell tongue-first into Elijah's face?"

"Fair enough. Look, I'm not trying to make excuses, but yesterday was rough for her. I came to grips with my parents' dysfunctional relationship a long time ago. But Hazy…she's taking it really hard." Simon paused. "Now Elijah, on the other hand. That guy's just an asshole."

Nara tried to stifle a laugh, but the effort was futile. She couldn't deny it brought her a small sense of release. But just as quickly, her laughter turned to tears. She knew

Simon must think she was crazy but right now she was helpless against the turbulence of her emotions.

"I'm sorry—I shouldn't have said that. I—"

Nara buried her head in his shoulder. She had no strength left for pretense. She was floundering, desperate for something or someone to latch on to. And Simon was there.

She was suddenly struck by a sober realization. Was this what Hazy had felt? Damaged, rejected, and alone? And Elijah—stupid, stupid Elijah—in the wrong place wrong place at the wrong time. But why hadn't Hazy come to her? Why had she put herself in a position to screw up so colossally?

Nara lifted her head from Simon's shoulder. "I'm sorry."

"No, it's okay. I mean, I don't—"

Nara stood and wiped the tears from her face with the sleeve of her hoodie. "You want to get out of here?" Her own words surprised her. She didn't know why she'd said it. She wasn't the type to cut class. She'd tried it once and learned her lesson.

"You mean, like…leave school?"

"You've got a car, right?"

"Yeah, but I've got a test later, and—"

Nara had already turned and started towards the parking lot. Was she running from her problems? Maybe. Or maybe for once in her life she was just going to let go and forget what everyone thought, consequences be damned. Caring had only gotten her hurt.

"Okay. What the hell? Let's do it," Simon said, catching up to her. "Where are we going?"

Half an hour later, Nara and Simon sat across from each other at Cooper's, a quaint coffee bar on the opposite side of town. Simon had suggested Pitch Black, the occult bookstore on Ridley Street. He had gushed over their "amazing lounge area with coffee-to-die-for," but Nara had gone her entire life without ever setting foot in that creepy place, and she wasn't about to start today. Thankfully, he had ultimately deferred to her.

"How many mirrors did you break? I mean, I've heard of bad luck but damn, Kilday."

Nara took a sip of her espresso. "Story of my life. I'm either completely invisible or in the spotlight for all the wrong reasons."

"Then you should probably never go into politics."

She chuckled. "Definitely not!"

Simon finished off his cup of black coffee and motioned to the waitress for a refill.

"What *do* you want to do?"

"You mean like for a career? I'm not sure. Probably a writer. That's what my dad says I should do anyway. He even gave me—" Nara stopped herself, unsure that this was a road she wanted to go down. But there was a part of her that was dying to unburden herself, to hear someone tell her she wasn't going crazy.

"Gave you what?" asked Simon.

"Oh, nothing. Never mind."

"Are you sure you're okay? Do you need me to take you home?"

"No, I'm fine," Nara replied, nervously glancing around the shop. There were only five or six other patrons, all absorbed with their books, laptops, and phones. She took a deep breath and considered a different approach. "What's your interest in the ruins? I mean, you seem to know a lot about them. I feel like there's a story there."

"It goes back to when I was a kid. My dad used to be a big reader, before he got sick. He always had lots of books lying around, mostly about weird subjects like ghosts, ESP, paranormal phenomena, stuff like that. He had this one about ancient cultures that had a chapter on the mystery of Darlington Hills. I must have been nine or ten when I first read it. It just blew my mind that there was something like that just a few miles from my house.

"So, yeah. Ever since then, I've been pretty much obsessed. Here, let me show you something." Simon reached into his book bag and pulled out a ragged, leatherbound notebook held together by duct tape. "This is my years of research—every book passage or newspaper article I could get my hands on, every crazy internet theory, including a few of my own—it's all here."

"It looks like it belongs in a museum! Is it okay if I touch it?"

"No, go for it. That thing's been through Hell and back. It can take it."

Nara opened the book to the creaking sound of old paper, tape, and leather. "It even sounds ancient! This is amazing. I can't believe I never knew this about you."

"Well, I've always tried to keep my more unconventional interests on the DL."

Nara laughed. "Simon, everyone knows you're a nerd."

"Okay, fine. But this isn't exactly the kind of thing you want to announce to the world, especially to, you know…girls."

Nara noticed his slight hesitation at the word "girls." She wondered whether she would have picked up on it if Hazy hadn't revealed his secret yesterday. But she had to admit—he had done a good job of hiding it, even now. That's assuming he still harbored any of those feelings. For all she knew, it had been just a youthful infatuation that had long passed.

Nara continued to flip through the pages, passing a series of articles about the rumored occult history of the ruins. "Do you think there's any truth to this stuff?"

"It seems to come up a lot. Some modern satanic symbology has been found out there, but most chalk that up to vandalism and kids playing around. But rumors persist but there are people who believe the ruins hold a more positive spiritual significance."

"Are you one of those people?"

"That's a complicated question. I definitely believe the ruins pre-date Native Americans by a few hundred if not thousands of years. But I'm not sure what their original purpose was. Why do you ask?"

Nara looked down at the swirling patterns in her cup. "I don't know. I heard some people talking today."

"Let me guess. Becca and Melani joined a secret cult?"

"Among other things, yeah. You don't think there's really anything to that, do you?"

Simon took a big swig of coffee. "In this town? It wouldn't be the craziest story I've heard."

"Okay, then. What is?"

Simon leaned in close. "You really want to know?"

"Of course!"

Josh Howard

"Okay. There's a theory..." He paused and scanned the room. "...that says that descendants of the original builders still exist, and they live somewhere deep in Veilwood Forest. And that they still practice the ancient ways of their ancestors. I'm talking about stuff outside the realm of known science."

"You mean witchcraft? Like real witchcraft with spells and sacrifices and stuff?"

"You asked for my craziest story."

"Fair enough."

Nara looked down at her backpack sitting at her feet beneath the table, the red cover of her journal visible through the gap in the faulty zipper. She wondered if there was something to Simon's stories. Nothing as outlandish as he was suggesting, of course. But something. She carefully considered her next words.

"Yesterday...out there. When I fell. What did you see?"

"Nothing really. I was talking, I heard Hazy trying to get your attention, then I looked over and you just seemed to freeze and fall over backwards."

"Anything else?"

"You were sort of reaching..." Simon said, demonstrating with his own arm, "...like you had been touching one of the stones."

"Seems pretty weird, right?"

"I really don't think you unleashed any hocus pocus or an ancient curse if that's what you're asking. I've been out there dozens of times and never experienced anything out of the ordinary—and not for lack of trying!"

Somehow Simon's attempt at reassurance only made her feel worse. She wasn't sure what she had hoped he would say, but she couldn't deny that there had to be something out there—some connection to what she was experiencing. Maybe there wasn't anyone or anything that was going to be able to provide her with answers. Maybe this was something she was going to have to face alone.

She continued thumbing through the pages of Simon's exhaustive research. Sensational headlines drew connections between the ruins and UFOs, zombies, and even Bigfoot. The collection of articles gave way to pages and pages of handwritten notes. Some of them appeared to be notes from Mr. Dargo's lectures. Then—

"...ara. Nara! Can you hear me?"

Simon was crouched over her, hands tight around her shoulders. The barista was next to her on the floor, wiping up a spill. The other patrons all stood around, staring down at her.

"Are you okay?" Simon asked, glasses askew in panicked concern. "You completely faded out and then slumped over. You looked like you were dead!"

"Do you need me to call you an ambulance?" the barista asked as she finished cleaning up Nara's spilled coffee.

Dread stirred in the pit of her stomach. "No. Simon, can you please take me home?"

"Of course!" he said, helping her up and then gathering his things.

As he closed up his notebook, Nara caught a glimpse of the last thing she must have seen before blacking out—two pages filled with sketches of the hieroglyphs and what appeared to be partial, rudimentary translations.

Nara hastily grabbed her backpack. One of its straps caught on the leg of her chair, spilling her books and papers in every direction.

"Oh, shit!" Simon said as he rushed to help. He grabbed a handful of homework papers, then went for Nara's journal, which lay splayed open to the pages of her bloody scribblings.

"Don't touch that!"

Simon froze.

The words had escaped from her lips before she could stop them. Utterly embarrassed, terrified, and ashamed, she grabbed her journal and ran out the front door.

CHAPTER 10

Nara sat huddled in a ball, hood up, arms wrapped firmly around her backpack. She faced the window, absently staring at the blur of passing of cars and street signs. However fast Simon was going, it wasn't fast enough. The only place she wanted to be right now was behind the locked door of her bedroom. The one place no one could embarrass or hurt her.

No one, maybe, except herself.

They rode in silence. Simon had gotten into the car and not said a word—she was grateful for that at least. Whatever had happened wasn't his fault, she knew. He had been nothing but kind and helpful. But she had let her guard down. In a moment of weakness, she had been dangerously close to opening up to him. And right now, she was too hurt, too raw to risk letting anyone get close.

They finally entered her neighborhood's subdivision. She ran scenarios through her head. Would she say goodbye? Thank you? Sorry for being a weirdo freak? Maybe she could save them both a lot of trouble by just opening the door and jumping out as he passed her house. She would gladly suffer a broken bone or two if it meant avoiding an awkward conversation.

A few blocks from home, Nara caught the familiar sight of Mrs. Pulaski out on her front lawn. But instead of pulling weeds or trimming bushes, she appeared to be strangely pouring out a bag of salt in a ring around her house. As they passed, the old woman stopped, stood up straight, and gave them a look that sent chills down Nara's spine.

The car pulled to a stop and Nara's heart sank. Her dad's squad car was in the driveway. She would have to explain why she wasn't in school. She considered telling Simon to keep driving, but quickly realized she wasn't going to solve one problem by exacerbating another. She reached for the door handle, but before she could decide on her choice of parting words, Simon broke the silence.

"I'm sorry if I did anything to embarrass you."

Damn, she thought. *This would be so much easier if he was a jerk.*

"It's fine. Don't worry about it." It came out colder than she intended. She opened the car door. "I'm sorry. I've just—"

"Had a run of shit luck. I get it. You don't have to apologize." He adjusted his glasses. "But if you need a friend, or just someone to listen, I'm here. I can write down my number. I'm not on any of the socials."

"No need. It's still in my phone from those sleepovers Hazy and I spent prank calling you from the next room."

"I remember. I don't think you guys realized I could hear you plotting through the vents."

"Oh, my God. I don't know how you put up with us. We were such huge dorks."

"And I was home alone on Friday nights. What did that say about me?"

And just like that, Nara realized he had done it again. Diffused the tension and brought her off the ledge. The guy who used to be Hazy's gross, dorky brother had somehow become sensitive and disarming when she hadn't been paying attention. She stepped from the car, shut the door, and leaned in through the open window. "Thank you. For the coffee and the ride. And for being cool." She turned and threw her backpack over her shoulder. When she reached the front door, she glanced back over her shoulder and met eyes with Simon as he pulled away.

Nara took a deep breath and opened the door. She was relieved to find her dad passed out on the couch and thanked God for that small bit of mercy. She quietly snuck past him and crept up the stairs, careful to avoid the creaky, loose boards of steps three and seven. Shutting the door to her room, she collapsed onto her bed. All she wanted was to close her eyes and forget about the world for a couple of hours.

She turned on her phone to set an alarm. Her lock screen showed notifications for fourteen text messages and three missed calls. The calls and two of the texts were from Hazy. Nothing from Elijah, of course. The rest were random numbers which she assumed were idiots from school harassing her over the morning's drama. She deleted those without even reading them.

Reluctantly, she opened the texts from Hazy.

The first one read: *I know there's nothing I can say to make this better. I fucked up and you have every right to hate me. I was weak. I was stupid. I went out looking for a way to numb my pain and put myself in a bad situation. It's*

*all my fault and I'll never forgive myself. I understand if our
friendship is over. But I want you to know I still love you.*
Then, *I need to hear from you. Tell me you hate me. Tell
me to go to Hell. I can live with anything but your silence.*

A thousand possible responses ran through her head,
but none of them seemed adequate. Hazy was already beat-
ing herself up about what happened. Was it right to just tear
into her and add to her misery? Maybe not, but was she
just supposed to hold back everything she felt? All Nara
knew for sure right then was that she just wanted to escape.
She placed her phone on the nightstand, rolled over, and
closed her eyes.

Nara dreamed. She was in school, walking down a
hallway. It was almost entirely dark, with only faint slivers
of moonlight creeping in through the windows. She passed
by a classroom that also seemed to be her bedroom. Inside,
Hazy and Elijah were locked in passionate lust, kissing,
groping, tearing at each other's clothes. Suddenly a man
was there at her side, someone she didn't recognize. He
was silent as he handed her a blade. Nara didn't feel rage
or anger or even sadness, just cold, calculated focus as she
walked over to Elijah and slit his throat. There was a wet,
gurgling sound as he gasped for air, his blood spurting out
all over Hazy as she screamed. Nara lifted her knife and
plunged it into Hazy's stomach. Again, and again. As the
life drained from Hazy's face, it changed to Britney's, then
her father's, then finally her own.

There was a shift, and Nara found herself looking up at
her emotionless, knife-wielding self through her own dying
eyes. Her other self was drenched in blood, her hair short-

er, her body covered in the ancient symbols as if she had carved them into her own flesh. The face of Nara's killer doppelgänger passed into shadow, and a realization hit her. This was the dream she'd had before, only now she knew the obscured face had been her own. She fell again through water and fire and finally darkness. She heard voices, both laughing and howling. She heard a child's cry and the whispers of a dying mother.

The cacophony gave way to the softer sounds of wind and the rustling of leaves. It was still nearly pitch black, but she knew where she was—in the forest, surrounded by the stone monuments. And she wasn't alone.

There was a cold presence in the dark—something watching, waiting in the shadows. She could feel the intensity of its gaze and the depravity of its intentions. A voice, both quiet and calamitous, uttered a single word.

"*Shadespawn.*"

She woke up.

The first thing Nara noticed, besides being drenched in sweat, was that it had happened again. Her journal lay open on her bed, page after page filled with new symbols freshly scrawled in her own blood. But there was more this time. Crude drawings of hideous faces and demonic forms. A map of the ruins, phases of the moon, and astrological configurations. And finally, across two pages, a diagram of a female figure, with three prominent symbols surrounding it.

A knock on her door punctuated the moment, nearly sending Nara out of her skin.

"You okay in there, sweetheart?"

She slammed the book shut and hurriedly shoved it in her backpack. She spat on her hand and tried scrubbing away the blood but it wasn't getting the job done fast enough. She panicked and pulled the sleeves of her hoodie down over her hands.

Her father knocked again. "Nara? Can we talk?"

Nara faked her best sick and pathetic voice. "It's unlocked."

Her dad opened the door, but remained standing in the hallway. "Hey, is everything okay? I got a call from school."

"Sorry, Dad. I'm not feeling well. I know I should have told someone but—"

"No, it's okay. I just wish you had called me."

"I didn't want to bother you. I know you're really busy."

"I'm never too busy for you. I feel like this is my fault. I should have insisted and taken you to the doctor yesterday."

"No, it's okay. I think it's just a stomach bug. Probably just need to let it run its course."

"I need to get back to the station soon, but I'm going to call Amanda and have her come over."

"Dad, no. Please. I'll be fine!"

"It's not up for discussion. I need this, for my own peace of mind. And…I think it's important you two start to get to know each other."

Nara didn't like the implication of that statement, and she knew this was not an argument she wasn't going to win. She sunk back into her pillow.

Her dad stepped into the room and sat down beside her on the bed. Nara tightly gripped the sleeves of her hoodie.

"How's everything else? School? The, uh…boyfriend situation?

"Not great."

"Elijah?"

"Yeah."

"I never did like that kid."

Nara desperately wanted to avoid going down this road and tried to steer the conversation in a different direction. "So, how goes the investigation?"

He sighed. "It's a tough one, maybe one of the toughest. My heart breaks for those families. We've definitely got our hands full. There's just too many facts that don't make sense."

She knew that was about as forthcoming as he was going to be, so she didn't press him.

He looked down at his phone. "I need to be getting back. Was there anything else?" he asked.

His tone suggested to Nara he was either stalling or digging for something. She glanced at her backpack lying at the foot of the bed. "No, just the usual."

She was relieved as he stood up and started for the door. Then he reached for the doorknob and stopped. The air grew tense. After a moment he turned back to face her.

"I heard you. Downstairs. You woke me up."

Nara's body went cold. Dread swelled in the pit of her stomach. "You...heard?

"You were screaming. It's happening again, isn't it? The dreams."

Nara swallowed hard. His words dredged deeply buried memories to the surface.

He rubbed his hands over his face. "Your mother and I...we prayed those days were over. How long has it been happening?"

"Just a couple of days." Her voice shook when she said it. This was the last thing she had wanted—for him to know, to put him through all that worry and fear all over again. She felt trapped with nowhere else to turn. How would she get through this without Mom? "Dad…I'm scared."

He wrapped his arms around her. "It's going to be okay, sweetheart. I promise."

Violent images from her dream flashed in her mind. "What if it's not? What if there's something wrong with me? What if—"

"No! I refuse to accept that. We'll get through this, just like we did last time."

"We had Mom last time." She had been the steadfast, faithful one, the one who made sure they said their prayers and were in church every Sunday. Dad had tried to fill the gap as best he could, but Nara knew that losing his wife had been a blow to his faith.

"And now she's watching over you. You're still our little girl, and we won't let this thing have you." His phone buzzed. "Damn it."

Nara wiped the tears from her eyes. "Work?"

"Yeah. But I'm not leaving until I know you're okay."

"I'll be fine. Those girls and their families need you right now."

"When things settle, we'll both sit down, talk about things. We'll figure this out. And I'm pretty sure I still owe you a birthday present," he said with the best grin he could muster.

She knew he was trying to lighten the moment, that he was more afraid than he was letting on. She played along and forced a smile. "Oh, I haven't forgotten."

"Didn't think so." He tussled her hair and kissed her forehead. "Amanda will be by in a bit to check on you. Credit card is in the usual spot if you want to order a pizza. And remember, keep the doors locked."

"I know, Dad."

"Love you, kid."

"Love you, too."

Nara listened as her father headed down the stairs, grabbed his keys, and went out the front door, locking it behind him. She waited until she heard the car start and back out of the driveway before she jumped off the bed, raced to his bedroom, and began rummaging through his closet. She knew it was hidden away in there somewhere.

They had called it The Box of Bad Dreams. Whenever she was little and had woken from one of her nightmares, her mom and dad would have her draw what she remembered, then condemn the drawing to The Box, where it would never trouble her again. She assumed they had read about the technique in some parenting book. It seemed like a good idea, but she couldn't say it was all that effective, considering the dreams had persisted for years.

She finally found it on the top shelf behind a stack of old jeans. The Box of Bad Dreams was in reality just an old beat-up shoe box that she had embellished with crayons and markers. She hesitated before removing the lid. She wasn't sure what she expected to find. She had little to no memory of the details of her past dreams or anything she actually drew and put in the box. Maybe in that sense, it had served its purpose.

She lifted the lid and noted the smell of old, dry paper. The first few drawings were practically indecipherable. She must have been around four years old when it had all started. But the images soon became more coherent, with drawings of a little girl crying in her bedroom, surrounded by monsters in the dark. But there was something else—a series of repetitive scribbles in the margins. Her heart raced. They seemed to be a match for the hieroglyphs as seen through the eyes of a child. She had been drawing them even then, before she had ever even been to the ruins.

She furiously dug through the rest of the box. The symbols appeared with increasing frequency as the drawings became more violent, with gory imagery of monsters attacking, her stabbing the monsters, and finally, a drawing of little Nara, knife in hand, standing over the dead bodies of her parents. Her stomach dropped. The very next drawing was almost exactly the same, but this time she was one of the dead bodies, and the killer had a blacked-out face.

She had no actual memories of those dreams, but the drawings didn't lie.

Something within her soul was dark and twisted.

It had always been there, and it wanted out.

CHAPTER 11

It had always been a mystery to her, exactly where she had come from. Whenever Nara had asked, her parents had always seemed to grow uncomfortable and change the subject. Their only answers had been things like "You were a gift from God" or "We didn't find you, you found us." She had only become more curious after she became a teenager and began to grow conscious of her lack of physical resemblance to either of them. She was sharp and angled where her mother was plump and well-rounded, and soft where her dad was square and chiseled. She had heard rumors at school—that her real parents had been criminals, possibly even murderers. Some had cruelly teased her about it. She had wanted to ask her parents if it was true, but she feared their answer. Could she live with knowing that her birth parents had done something horrific? She had put all her remaining curiosity aside when Mom got sick. She had felt guilty and selfish to dwell on it at that point. But now, the desire to know burned stronger than ever. She couldn't help but wonder if there was something in her past that could help her better understand herself and what was happening to her. But that particular avenue of exploration would have to wait for now.

"This is crazy," she said out loud for the third time as she shoved her journal into her backpack. She quickly tied her hair up into a ponytail and paused in front of her bedroom mirror. Her auburn hair, blue eyes, light smattering of freckles, and slender frame hadn't changed, but something inside her had. She feared she was on the verge of losing herself.

But she refused to surrender to those thoughts. How could she ever hope to stand against anyone or anything if she didn't finally confront the tyranny of her own secret darkness? Nara knew it was time to stop running. From conflict. From herself.

Her phone buzzed—a text from Simon, letting her know he was waiting out front. When he had texted an hour ago to check on her, asking if he could bring her anything, her first instinct was to close up and blow him off. But Nara had begun to realize she wasn't going to get through this alone. She needed someone to confide in. With things the way they were with Hazy, and her dad wrapped up in work, that didn't leave many options. And truthfully, there was part of her that wanted to open up to Simon, whatever that meant.

Plus, he had been pretty insistent, refusing to take no for an answer.

She slipped into her hoodie and slung her backpack over her shoulder, hurrying down the stairs. She stopped by the kitchen, briefly contemplating leaving a note. If Dad came home to find her gone, he'd be livid. Nothing she could write would change that. She would just have to take her chances.

She opened the front door and yelped. Amanda stood there, just as startled. In her spontaneity, Nara had forgotten one important detail.

"My Lord! You scared me half to death, sweetheart! Your father probably didn't tell you, but he's worried sick. He asked me to come by and check on you."

In the span of about five seconds, Nara's mind constructed and dismissed about a dozen different explanations and excuses for why she was fully dressed, wearing her backpack, and on her way out the door to a waiting car. Each was more ridiculous and elaborate than the last. There was no way out. She was busted.

"Um…yeah, hey. You see—"

Amanda looked over her shoulder to where Simon's car sat idling by the curb. "I think I know what's going on here."

"It's not…I'm just—"

"It's okay. I was young once too. Don't worry, it'll be our secret. Go on, have a good time. Just not *too* good a time." She winked.

Nara was stunned. Amanda was actually…cool? "Really, it's not what you think. There's just a thing…"

Amanda grinned. "Get out of here, kid. I'll cover for you."

Nara decided not to push her luck. "Thank you, Amanda. I owe you." She crossed the lawn and looked back over her shoulder, waving at Amanda as she got into Simon's car.

"Hey. What was that all about?"

Amanda stood in the doorway, still watching and waving.

"Just drive," Nara said.

"Where to? You hungry?"

"Just somewhere we can talk."

The car pulled away, and Nara looked back at her house, hoping she wasn't making a huge mistake.

Nara fidgeted with the wrapper of her half-eaten burger. After spilling her guts, her appetite had vanished.

"I knew it. You think I'm crazy."

"No."

"Then why'd you get so quiet?"

"Just thinking. Can I...see it?

"Do you always use that line when sitting in a parked car with a girl?"

He grinned, his face bathed in red light from the giant neon gorilla on the Burger Kong sign. "First time, actually."

Nara, struck by the absurdity of revealing her darkest secrets in the parking lot of a fast-food joint, reached into her backpack and produced the journal. She hesitated, rubbing her thumb over its leather surface. Once she did this, there was no turning back. "So, this...this is why I sort of freaked out on you at the coffee shop."

"I'm not going to judge you, Nara, if that's what you're afraid of. I mean, you've already seen my own 'Book of Crazy.'"

"Fair point, I guess." She took a deep breath, handed him the journal, and anxiously watched him turn through the pages with calm, focused intensity.

For several moments, he didn't say a word. Nara turned and stared out the window, growing more uncomfortable by the minute, wishing she could be anywhere else.

"Incredible," he finally said. "I mean, pretty twisted that you did this in your own blood. But incredible!"

"What do you mean *incredible?*"

"Nara...there's nearly a whole alphabet here. There are things here that are not on any of the stones. You've filled in almost all the missing pieces! How did you do this?"

"I told you. I don't know. I'm not in control when it happens."

"And you said this happened when you were a kid too?"

She pulled out a couple of the drawings she had taken from the Box of Bad Dreams. "What do you think it all means?"

"I don't know. You say you've never been to the ruins before yesterday?"

"Not that I remember, no. But something happened when I touched that stone. I think it unlocked something in my brain, like a repressed memory. Or it opened me up to some force or power. I'm scared, Simon. I don't understand what's happening to me."

"Let's go."

"Where?"

"To the forest. The ruins."

"What? Now?"

"Nara, with what you have here, we might be able to finally translate what's written on the stones. And maybe... maybe even find some answers for you."

Any other day, any other time, Nara's answer would have been a resounding and definite "No."

But not today.

"Okay. Let's do it."

Less than five minutes on the road to Veilwood, Nara was already second guessing herself. Maybe she would just tell him to drive her home and forget the whole thing. Going out into the woods after sundown to look at some old rocks while there was a potential killer on the loose? It was crazy.

Doubt continued to hammer at her resolve in the dense, contained silence of Simon's car until a synthy ringtone broke the silence. Simon reached into his jacket pocket while keeping one hand on the wheel. He glanced down at his phone, silenced it, and quickly returned it to his pocket.

"Everything okay?"

"Yeah, yeah. Fine. Just um…Mom. She's just…you know…"

Nara noticed his hands tighten around the steering wheel. "You can just take me home if you need to deal with that. I understand."

"No. No, it's fine. This is important. We're doing this!"

Nara heard the pain behind his feigned excitement. He needed a friend tonight as much as she did. This whole ridiculous excursion was probably just a way to distract himself from facing his own nightmares. He had told her he had come to terms with it, but she realized now that he'd been putting on a brave face. It was then that she decided. Once she got home, she would finally call Hazy and begin the process of trying to mend their friendship.

CHAPTER 12

"Veilwood Forest National Park. Closed. Reopens at 7 a.m." read the entry sign over the locked gate. Simon, undeterred, pulled the car off onto the shoulder and put it into park.

"So, what now?" Nara said.

"Oh, don't worry about that. I've been out here dozens of times after dark. I know a couple of the rangers. They're good dudes." Simon removed the keys from the ignition and pulled out a flashlight from the center console, flicking it on and off to test the batteries. "All right. Let's go!" he said, exiting the car. "And don't forget the journal!"

Nara stepped outside, throwing her backpack over her shoulder. "I can't believe I'm actually doing this."

Simon jumped the waist-high wooden fence several yards down from the main gate. Nara followed, taking Simon's hand as she climbed over. Was it her imagination, or did he seem to hold on to her hand for a second or two longer than necessary? Nara wasn't sure how it made her feel. The idea that Simon might have had a thing for her was still new. The strangest thing of all, though, was that she was discovering that maybe she wasn't as weirded out by the idea as she was a little over twenty-four hours ago.

Simon activated his flashlight and started down the main trail, moving with intensity and purpose. The air was cool, the moon full and high overhead, its light struggling to penetrate the dense canopy of the forest. All was deathly silent save for the occasional snapping twig or crunch of leaves. Reality set in. They were alone, in the dark of the wild, and if anything happened, no one knew where she was. Nara felt her anxiety rise. She struggled to keep up with Simon's pace as the ground grew more treacherous, limbs and branches clawing and scraping at her face and clothes. They had clearly left the main path. She could barely make out the beam from his flashlight anymore.

"Hey! Hold up! Some of us don't exactly know our way around here."

She faintly heard the ring of his phone again and he stopped—but for her sake or for the phone, she couldn't say. He appeared to type a quick text and then placed it back in his jacket pocket.

"Hey!" she called again. Had he even heard her?

"Huh? Oh, sorry."

Nara was close enough to see his face now. He was drenched in sweat.

"I get lost in my own head sometimes," he said, catching his breath. "You okay?"

"Yeah. Listen, maybe we should call this off. Maybe come back tomorrow during the day?"

"What? No, we're almost there! Here." He pulled a bottle of water from his backpack. "I meant to give this to you earlier."

"I'm good," she said, her frustration rising.

"I don't want you getting dehydrated and fainting on me again."

Nara took a drink and handed it back. "Look, there's really no reason we have to do this tonight. I was stupid to agree to it in the first place. If my dad—"

"Shhh!" he interrupted, putting his finger to his lips. He turned, looking, listening. "Did you hear that?"

"No, I—"

He held up his hand, motioning her to keep quiet. She was at her wit's end. Fumbling around in the dark alone was one thing, but if someone or something was out there with them, that was it. She wasn't about to risk her life over this. She didn't care what else Simon had to say.

She just was about to demand he take her home when she heard it.

Laughing.

Simon motioned for her to follow him. Thankfully, this time he stayed slow and close. When he finally stopped, he crouched down behind a large mound of uniformly stacked rocks. They had just reached the edge of the ruins.

Simon pointed and whispered, "Right over there. See it?"

She couldn't miss it. Their destination was about fifty yards ahead, illuminated by the glow of a fire. Its light flickered across the large standing stones and through the surrounding thicket. Voices laughed. Bodies danced. It was a party.

"Typical. Probably a bunch of dumb jocks and preps."

"Now can we go?"

"I hate to come all this way to leave empty handed. Let me check it out first. Stay here, just to be safe. You never know if one of these idiots is packing."

"Simon!"

"I'll be right back, I promise."

He leaped over the pile of stones, and within seconds, he'd vanished into the dark. Nara's frustration with Simon was now nearing Elijah levels of irritation. She just wanted to go home. She looked and listened for any sign of Simon reaching the party, but it was too far to really make out any actual conversation or discern one silhouetted form from another. Even in the dark with the rough terrain, it shouldn't take him more than a minute or two to reach them.

Nara leaned her head back against the cold stones and closed her eyes. She took a deep breath and tried to calm herself by rubbing her fingers back and forth over the smooth outer edge of her necklace. She whispered a few words of prayer, but they came out forced and hollow. Even in her distressed state, she couldn't muster the strength for a sincere plea for divine intervention. The last couple of days had taken their toll. She had never felt so isolated and detached from what she believed. Never felt so alone.

Moments felt like hours. Nara shivered, huddling against the stones to block the sudden chill breeze. She looked up just in time to see the slow but steady advance of a dark thunderhead obscure the moon. A single wet drop tapped her on the cheek. Perfect. Just perfect.

She pulled her phone from her pocket and briefly contemplated texting someone—anyone—to come and rescue her. Then everything went deathly still. Even the distant sound of raucous voices had gone quiet. Moments passed. A lone twig snapped, breaking the silence. Then another. Her heart raced. She wasn't alone. She looked down at her screen, careful to keep its light from giving her away and quickly texted Simon.

Where r u??? Pls hurry!

She waited. And waited. Seconds stretched into eternity. Another drop splashed across her screen.

Simon!!

She wasn't going to wait to be prey for whatever was out there. She slowly stood, careful not to make any noise or sudden movements. She had to try and make a dash for the party. She didn't care who they were at this point—safety in numbers.

It was then she felt her cheeks go warm, and the forest seemed to shift. Her knees wobbled. Something was wrong. She leaned onto the pile of stones for stability, and her vision blurred. From somewhere behind her, sounds of snapping and cracking echoed in her ears, announcing the arrival of her stalker in the dark. She watched as a shape emerged from the trees, as black as the night itself, only the faint glow of the moon giving edges to its form. Nara turned to run only to be met by the sudden impact of the cold hard ground. Her legs had failed her.

She pushed herself up and lurched forward, her body slow and sluggish to respond to her brain's commands. Stumbling ahead, she kept her focus on the light of the fire, slowly gaining ground as her adrenaline surged. But the forest was without mercy. Twisted limbs ripped and tore at her clothes and flesh. She tripped again, landing hard on an exposed root, knocking the wind out of her. She rolled over, struggling to breathe while trying to catch a glimpse of her pursuer. But between her blurred vision and the absence of moonlight, she was as good as blind. She forced herself up and made a final, desperate dash for the potential refuge of the bright orange glow ahead.

CHAPTER 13

Nara burst through the surrounding trees into the circle of stones. The fire raged at the foot of the central altar stone as people casually milled about, talking, laughing, and drinking, completely oblivious to her intrusion. She scanned the crowd, hoping to find someone she recognized. Simon. Where was Simon?

"Hello…there's someone out there…someone trying to—" the words came out heavy and slurred. The forest was spinning, and she fought to keep her balance. What was happening to her? Was it something she ate? Or was it the forest—the stones themselves, once again casting some bizarre spell on her body? Her insides lurched. She doubled over and vomited.

"Holy shit! Nara Kilday!"

Even in her impaired state, Nara knew that voice. It was the bane of her existence.

"What the hell are you doing out here?" asked Britney as others began to gather around.

Nara scanned their faces. Some seemed familiar—Violet and Heather of course, and others, but it was getting harder to focus…to think. Where was Simon?

"Simon? Sweetie, I think you're lost."

Laughter erupted from the blur of faces. Nara hadn't realized she had asked for Simon out loud. But he wasn't here. Had he gotten lost, fallen somewhere? Abandoned her? Whatever had happened, she was alone. Only one option was left, and it was the last thing she wanted to do. She reached for her phone, ready to dial her father, but felt a hand clamp tight around her wrist.

"I don't think so." Britney grabbed Nara's phone and tossed it into the woods.

"No!"

"Who's going to save you now, Kilday? Your best friend is hooking up with the only guy who ever gave you the time of day. That's really gotta burn."

Laughter and cheers rose from the crowd.

"Kick her ass!"

"Fight! Fight! Fight!"

Nara clutched the sides of her head. The chanting reverberated in her brain like a pounding drum.

"Rumor is that you're still a virgin. Maybe if you'd given it up, Elijah wouldn't have had to get it somewhere else. God knows Hazy's never said no to anyone."

More laughter. The wind picked up, bringing with it the sound of distant thunder.

Britney stepped closer to Nara, only inches from her face. She raised her cup and poured ice cold beer out onto Nara's head. "That's for ruining my dress."

Nara's old companions, shame and humiliation, reared their ugly heads, but she wouldn't succumb to their power, not this time. Nara drew upon something else. Something stronger, darker. Something Nara had long fought to keep at bay.

Rage.

"Let's see what you've got in there." Nara felt a hard tug as someone ripped her backpack from her body and tossed it to Britney. The girl smirked as she emptied it out onto the ground.

"Oooh, what's this?" Violet went immediately for the journal.

Nara fumed through gritted teeth. "Don't. Touch. That."

"Someone's mad!" Britney played to the mocking crowd.

Violet was already combing through the journal. "Holy shit! You've got to see this, Britney!"

Her eyes widened as she scanned its pages.

Nara—wet, cold, and shivering—balled her fists. "Give it back!"

"What kind of messed up shit are you into? So much for the sweet Christian girl act. It's always the ones who pretend to be holier than thou that are the real sick freaks."

Nara surrendered to the rage. Reality was a blur, moving faster than she could process while her own body seemed to move in slow motion. She stood outside her own skin, watching herself furiously slam her fists into Britney's perfect little face. Within seconds, or maybe minutes, hands were grabbing her, pulling her off, holding her back. Normal time seemed to resume. Britney stood, wiping blood from her nose and swollen lips. She raised a finger at Nara.

"You freak bitch! You're going to pay for that!"

"What the hell is going on here!" a stern voice boomed from the dark. Everything stopped but the rustle of wind and leaves. Out of the shadows materialized an imposing but welcoming presence.

"Mister Dargo!"

The panic and fear in Britney's voice was palpable.

Dargo pointed to the crowd. "Let her go!"

Nara fell to her knees as her restrainers released their hold on her. The adrenaline-fueled rage subsided, leaving her feeling even weaker than before.

"She came here just to start shit, Mister Dargo!"

"I don't want to hear it! This behavior is completely unacceptable. There is a way we do things, and this isn't it. Collect your things and go. We will discuss disciplinary action later."

The crowd began to obediently file out without protest. Nara crawled on her hands and knees gathering her stuff back into her backpack, but her journal was nowhere to be found.

Thunder roared overhead as Mr. Dargo observed the students file out one by one, disappearing into the forest. They were finally alone except for the foreboding quiet presence of the stones. Before she knew it, he was at her side, helping her to her feet. "Are you injured?"

"No...no. Just a little...dizzy. Thank you...thank you so much, Mister Dargo. I'm so glad you're here."

He then looked away from her and into the dark. He remained still, watching...waiting? Then something moved. Nara gripped Dargo's arm, startled. Two black shapes seemed to coalesce from the darkness and shift forward in their direction. "Mister Dargo!"

"It's okay, Nara," he said with unnatural calm.

The illumination of the fire gave form to the advancing shapes—two figures in hooded black robes, faces hidden in shadow. Dargo's own face seemed to darken. "Take her."

"What? No!" Nara turned to run but they already had her. She gave everything she had left, thrashing and flailing. But it was hopeless. Impaired or not, they were bigger and stronger. They slammed her onto the altar and began binding her feet and wrists to the stone. She screamed. "Simon! Somebody! Help!"

Flames danced behind Dargo as he stood at the foot of the altar, donning his own black robe. He turned, raised his arms, and several more hooded figures stepped out from the darkness in unison. Nara screamed again for Simon. Thunder, violent and heavy, roared as if in response.

"What once was taken, has been returned," Dargo spoke, projecting his voice over the crash of thunder and the crackle of fire. "What has ascended, will now descend. Spirit to flesh. Flesh to damnation. Holy abomination."

Nara's vision swam, her limbs went numb, and she began to pass in and out of consciousness. Reality became dim and indistinct. Time stopped and sped up. The robed ones began to chant. Dargo was at her feet, then suddenly at her side. He held something—it glinted in the firelight. A dagger, long and curved. She felt the force of his hand on her, pressing her face hard into the stone, then a sharp tug at the back of her head. When her eyes opened again, he was raising his hands high, knife in one, clump of hair in the other. Her ponytail?

"Daughter of darkness. Soultorn. Bloodcursed. Shadespawn."

Those haunting words.

Dargo tossed the bundle of hair into the fire. It erupted with fury. From deep within the forest, a scream, shrill and terrible, pierced the night. Then Nara lost the battle with herself, and everything went black.

She was nowhere and everywhere at once. She saw Hazy, lying on her bed, in tears. Her father, alone in his office, head in his hands. Elijah plucking at his guitar. Her mother, sitting on the foot of Nara's bed, sun shining brightly through the window behind her.

"Mom?" Nara sat up. She rubbed her eyes. "Is it really you?"

"*Talitha koum*! Time to wake up."

Nara leaned forward and embraced her mother. It had annoyed her then, but how she missed hearing her mother routinely greet her with the same two words every morning. "Oh, Mom. I missed you so much! Please don't leave me again!"

Her mother pushed her away, and the smile evaporated from her face.

"It's time to get up, Nara. Get up now!"

"Mom?"

She became furious. "Get up, Nara! Now!"

Nara returned to reality just in time to see Dargo raising his dagger high above his head, eyes closed, chanting. She was instantly aware of the ice-cold wind across her skin and looked down to see that her clothes had been removed down to her underwear, her body covered in red symbols, written presumably in her own blood. Dargo finished his unholy chant and opened his eyes, then brought the knife down.

At that moment, from somewhere deep within her soul, Nara screamed, and all at once, several things happened: lightning flashed, the fire died, rain poured, and the stone altar spit in two, freeing Nara from her bonds and causing Dargo to miss his target.

Nara didn't waste a second. Before anyone had realized what had happened, she was already away, darting blindly into the woods—cold, wet, no clothes, no light, no direction, just pure will to escape and survive. She gave no regard to pain as her bare feet sped over rocks and limbs. She had no idea if she was going in the right direction; she just had to get away.

Lightning flashed and for a moment Nara got a look at her surroundings. Nothing looked familiar, but a reflective glint caught her eye. She ran towards it and fell to her hands and knees, grasping in the dark. Lightning flashed again and there it was. Her phone. As she reached for it, she was caught in the beam of a flashlight.

A voiced shouted. "Over here!"

Nara grabbed the phone and resumed her escape. She heard shouting as they all converged in her direction. For about half a second, she considered activating the phone's flashlight to aid her escape, but that would only help to give her away. She just needed a moment—needed to get far enough away, hide long enough to get a text out to her dad, Simon, anyone. *Simon*. God, where was he? Had they gotten him too? She had little doubt now what fate had befallen Becca and Melani.

She made the mistake of glancing over her shoulder to try to get a glimpse of her pursuers. Her foot caught on God knows what, sending her tumbling through the air, landing hard onto craggy rocks and sharp foliage. She rolled violently down a steep incline, tossing end over end, elbows and knees striking every jagged edge on the way down.

When she finally came to a stop, it took everything in her to keep from crying out in agony. Her head pounded, and her body stung from the pain of a hundred cuts and scrapes. Most painful of all, she had lost her phone again in the fall.

She lay in the cold, wet mud for what felt like an eternity, trying to catch her breath and terrified to move. If her pursuers were close, they were being stealthy about it. The forest had grown deathly quiet except for the slow patter of rain which was becoming steadier by the minute. She had to get up. She had to move. Had to find her phone. If she stayed put, she would die, by the elements if nothing else.

She tried to stand and instantly collapsed to her knees from the pain lancing up her leg, likely broken. That was going to be a problem. She tried standing again, and bit her lip to keep from screaming. She had no idea how she was going to keep going.

Traversing the tangled forest in the dark of night was near impossible as it was.

She thought of her mother. Had it been a dream? A delirious hallucination? It didn't matter. Her mother had appeared to her. Saved her life. Told her to run. "*Talitha koum*," she had said, like she had used to say to her every morning. An Aramaic phrase from the book of Mark that plainly meant, "little girl, arise."

"*Talitha koum*," Nara muttered aloud to herself. She wasn't going to give up. Her mother didn't save her only for her to die out in the mud, broken and afraid. She would crawl out on her hands and knees if she had to. That's when she saw it—a bright light shining out of the dark only a few feet ahead, followed by a familiar vibrating tone. She had found her phone, and she was getting a call.

She hobbled forward then went down on all fours, scrambling to reach it before the call dropped. She was too late, but it had been her dad. She instantly dialed back but it went straight to voicemail. Nara swore in frustration. She tried again. Voicemail. It might be her only chance. "Dad! They're trying to kill me! Veilwood—" The call dropped before she could even finish.

"There she is!"

Nara was blinded by the beam of a flashlight. She ran. Pain, cold, pouring rain, none of it mattered. She just had to keep going, one agonizing step after another. Voices shouted behind her. They were splitting up, trying to triangulate her position. She tried to keep her path unpredictable, weaving right and left. She knew she was playing a dangerous game. One misstep could mean another fall—potentially her last.

If she could just make her way back to the parking lot...but finding the trail seemed hopeless. She ducked behind a tree and dialed her father again. Voicemail again. She prayed that meant he had gotten her message and was already on his way to her.

It had grown quiet again. The voices had stopped. Something didn't feel right. She had a sense they were near, closing in, surrounding her. Emotions swelled. Even if her father were on his way, he would never make it in time. Her only hope now was Simon, if he was still alive and hadn't abandoned her. Knowing that the slightest movement or sound risked giving her away, she took a deep, shivering breath and dialed him.

In the eerie silence, Nara heard the chime of a familiar synthy ringtone. It was close. She stood up and stepped out from behind the outcropping.

One of the cultists stood just a few feet away, illuminated by a phone screen as the ringtone continued to play.

He silenced the phone and removed his hood.

Nara felt the blood drain from her face.

From off to her right, a voice called out, "Over here!"

Nara turned and ran.

No, no, no, no, no. No! The words reverberated through her mind over and over again. *No, no, no! It can't be.* She pressed on, struggling through the pain of her broken body and spirit, but the pain of her injured leg reasserted itself with a vengeance. Her determined run to freedom degenerated into a defeated hobble.

Nara stopped at the sound of rushing water. She used the light from her phone to get a better look at her surroundings. She had come to the edge of a steep ravine that led down to a raging river. This was the end of the line.

With nothing to lose, she quickly dialed her father again, but the call failed to go through. She thought of Hazy. Her best friend in the whole world. Now their fallout seemed so small, so insignificant. She wished she had made things right when she'd had the chance.

Someone burst through the brush behind her. She turned around, and there he was. She was unprepared for the anguish she saw on his face. A thousand questions came to her mind, but the only one that came out was, "Why?"

Simon clenched his jaw and swallowed hard. "I'm sorry."

Another cultist emerged from the woods. "Over here! We've got her!"

In that moment, Simon stepped forward and drove a knife into Nara's belly.

Then again.

And again.

Surprisingly painless, but cold. As the life drained from her body, Nara's last thought was of her mother.

Her lifeless body fell backwards off the edge of ravine and into the turbulent, icy river below.

CHAPTER 14

Hazy was in Hell.

Another day, another ten hours of angry customers, piss-poor tips, aching feet, and sore back, all so she could try and fill the economic hole left by her mother running out on them. Hazy barely made enough to cover the rent and medication for her dad, much less food, electricity, and everything else. She couldn't even rely on her brother, who had become increasingly erratic and absent from her life. She had no idea where the hell Simon disappeared to for days and weeks at a time and had given up even asking. Hazy had endured a world of shit too, but she couldn't afford to check out. Not now. Someone had to keep everything from spinning completely out of control. But after nearly three months of this, working every extra shift she could get, all through the weekend and every day after school, managing the house, her dad's failing health, and still coming up short, she was worn out.

With each passing day, her hatred for her mother grew. She hated her for doing this to them. Hated her for bailing when Hazy had needed her the most. Last she had heard, Mom was somewhere in Florida, living it up with her boyfriend and his two daughters while her own flesh and blood drowned in her wreckage. Hazy's only solace was that she knew, eventually, her mother would find some way to completely ruin that too. Hazy held malicious hopes to one day see her mother crawling back for forgiveness, only so she could slam the door in her face.

The worst part was, no matter how much Hazy promised herself she would never be like her—would never betray the people she most cared about—she knew the truth. It was already too late. Not only had she betrayed the one person in the world she was closest to, Hazy was convinced that her actions had led, in some way, to Nara's disappearance. Directly or indirectly, it didn't matter. Hazy was responsible, and no one would convince her otherwise. Maybe Hell was just what she deserved.

Jack sat alone at his usual table, sipping his coffee, and reading the paper. It was a quarter past midnight—closing time—and he didn't seem to be in any hurry. He was their newest regular, his first visit a few weeks back as far as anyone could remember. Jack's name wasn't Jack, that's just what Hazy had come to call him in her mind. It was short for lumberjack, on account of his dark, shaggy beard, and the abundance of red plaid shirts he seemed to own. She had no idea what his real name was. He wasn't much for conversation and always paid in cash. Truthfully, despite his appearance, he didn't give off the vibe of someone who worked outdoors. His hands and clothes were too clean to be coming off a job, and he was always reading and never in a rush. With his lean form, dark hair, and blue eyes, Hazy might even find him a little handsome if he wasn't probably twice her age.

She made another pass by his table, hoping this time he would get the hint. "Sure there isn't anything else I can get you?"

"No, I'm good. Thank you," he said without even looking up from his newspaper.

It was all Hazy could do not to sigh and storm off. All she wanted at this moment was to go home and wash the day off. Instead, she started her slow march back to the kitchen. Just as she was contemplating putting herself out of her own misery by slamming her head in the refrigerator door, "Jack" called her back.

"I'm so sorry. You probably want to get out of here, don't you? I tend to get too wrapped up in what I'm doing, lose track of time. Bring me the check and I'll get out of your hair."

Hazy had the check on the table before he even finished talking, slapping it down only slightly harder than she intended. Jack raised his eyebrows and neatly (and annoyingly) folded up his newspaper, front page up, before reaching for his wallet. "Vipers Strike Again! Darlington High Headed to Playoffs!" blared the headline. Below that, a story about a cheerleader fundraiser and a brief mention of Sheriff Kilday being under fire for his handling of the investigation into the disappearances of Nara, Becca, and Melani. Besides that, there was no mention of the girls.

"You okay?" Jack asked.

If Hazy had made a face or shown any kind of reaction, she hadn't realized it. He handed her two twenties, over twice what he owed. "Keep the change. You look like you've had a long day."

Hazy bit her tongue.

Jack stood up and grabbed his green fleece jacket as Hazy began clearing the table. "Damned shame isn't it?" he said.

Why won't you just leave already? Hazy wasn't in the mood for conversation, but she did appreciate the generous tip. "What's that?"

"Those girls. It's like the whole town has already moved on."

Hazy momentarily paused her vigorous wipe down of the table. "Yeah. It's bullshit."

"Kind of makes you wonder, doesn't it?" He slid his arms into his jacket and raised the collar. "Good night, Hazy," he said, glancing at her name tag before turning and walking out the front door.

What the hell was that all about?

Twenty minutes later, Hazy was finally on her way home in her red hatchback clunker, too exhausted to even turn on the radio. She drove with the window down, hoping to mitigate the accumulated smell of grease, fried food, and sweat. Her hair fluttered wildly in the wind, having grown long and uneven since haircuts had become a luxury she could no longer afford.

Her thoughts returned to Nara, as they did every night on her way home. Hazy held out hope that she was still out there, alive and safe. She liked to imagine that Nara had just had enough of it all and started a new life somewhere. She couldn't say she would have blamed her. But with each day that passed, a little more hope faded. If the police were making any headway in the case, they weren't saying. According to the them, the big link between all three girls, besides their ages, was the fact that they had all been adopted.

But that had only provoked more questions than answers. It seemed everyone in Darlington Hills had their own pet theory as to what happened to the girls, the more salacious the better. Accusations ranging from indifference to favoritism had been hurled at Sheriff Kilday, with some even suggesting that he was somehow involved. Hazy couldn't imagine the nightmare he must be going through.

She continued on her usual route, all the way down Freemont, over the bridge, and past Morrell's 24 Hour Pharmacy, but a car accident forced her to take a detour down MacArthur, right past the north entrance to Darlington High.

She came to a stop at the red light, right next to the DHH marquee, where a makeshift memorial had been set up for the missing girls. It had looked nice for the first couple of weeks, when students would regularly bring flowers and signs and hold candlelight vigils, but all that had passed. The pictures and signs had faded, and the flowers were long dead. Nara deserved better.

After a quick trip to Morrell's Pharmacy, Hazy returned with a fresh bouquet, some poster board, and a black Sharpie, all bought with the extra tip money from Jack. She pulled into the parking lot and wrote out "Not Forgotten! Love and miss you, Nara. Come home safe!" on the poster board in large block letters. After some quick tidying of the memorial, she placed the sign and flowers beneath Nara's faded photograph. She'd have to come back soon to replace that too.

"It looks nice."

Startled, Hazy twisted around to see that last person in the world she expected.

"Damn it, Britney!"

"Sorry, I didn't mean to scare you," she said, habitually tucking a lock of hair behind her left ear.

"What the hell are you doing out here?" Hazy clenched her fists. One cross word about Nara and she was ready to throw down.

Britney looked around nervously. "I don't know."

Something wasn't right. This wasn't the Britney Hazy knew. Sure, she had kept her distance ever since Nara's disappearance, either out of total shame, or maybe even common human decency. But this...this seemed different. The girl seemed rattled.

"I was driving by and saw you out here. I just thought..."

"Thought what? You made Nara's life a living hell. She never did a damn thing to you. I hope you feel like shit now, I really do. But you've had three months to say something...anything. So, forgive me if I don't want to hear a word you have to say right now." Hazy turned and started towards her car.

"Wait! Please!"

Hazy stopped, turned, and pointed her finger directly at Britney. "I swear to God, the next words out of your mouth better be—"

"I'm sorry," she said, cutting her off. "I really, really am."

Was Hazy seeing things? Were those tears in her eyes?

"Don't you dare. You have no right to cry, bitch."

Britney wiped her eyes. "No, you're right. You're right. What I've done..."

"Save it, okay?" Hazy resumed her march back to her car.

"Be careful. They're watching. Always watching."

Hazy stopped, but didn't bother turning around this time.

Britney continued. "Me. You especially. Your brother…"

Hazy looked over her shoulder to see Britney looking off into the dark. "What about my brother?"

Britney's eyes darted back and forth. "I've got to go," she said and disappeared around the corner, leaving Hazy shocked, angry, a little creeped out, and thoroughly confused.

CHAPTER 15

As Hazy pulled up to the last trailer in the lot of Twin Points Trailer Park, she was surprised to see Simon's beat-up blue sedan parked out front. It had to have been at least two weeks since she saw him last, and even then, it had only been for a moment as he made some hurried excuse and was on his way again. That's why it was an even bigger shock to find him resting comfortably on the couch next to Dad, both enjoying fast food and watching some ridiculously loud movie featuring gratuitous explosions.

Hazy let the screen door slam behind her. "Can you please turn that down?" If either of them saw or heard her come in, they didn't acknowledge it. "Hello?" She threw her keys at Simon, missing and hitting the wall behind him. He jumped and reached for the remote, pausing the movie.

"Jeez! What the hell, Hazy?"

"You trying to get the cops called on us? It's nearly two a.m.! And what is he doing up?" She gestured to her father.

"We're just enjoying a movie. Calm down."

"Calm down? I'm the one running him back and forth to the doctor while you're out doing God knows what. He needs his rest. Come on, Dad. You're going to bed." She grabbed him by the arm, gently helping him up from the couch.

"I wanna finish the movie," he said, seemingly un-aware of the conversation that had just taken place in front of him. Max Foss was in his early fifties, but ever since his health had taken a dive, he could easily pass for someone nearly two decades older. The decline had begun a couple of years ago, and it seemed like none of the doctors they had taken him to could provide a clear answer. Their only solution had been to medicate his symptoms, to the point where Hazy could no longer tell the sickness from the side effects. He had never been the best father. He could be de-tached, insensitive, and a little mean when drunk, but Hazy would have given anything to have that version back over what he had deteriorated into.

"You can finish the movie tomorrow."

"Goodnight, Dad. See you in the morning," Simon said.

Hazy returned moments later, having successfully got-ten her father in bed without too much resistance. Simon had remained sitting on the couch, scrolling through his phone.

"Was all that really necessary?" he said without looking up.

"What do you think you're doing?"

"I was trying to spend some quality time with Dad."

"You want to spend quality time with Dad? You could start by maybe taking him to an appointment or two, or maybe filling his prescriptions and making sure he stays fed! Do you know that I wake up three times a night to make sure he hasn't died in his sleep? I'm worn out, Si-mon! I could use some goddamned help!"

"Didn't you get the money I left last week?"

"Oh, gee. Thanks. That hundred bucks was a real game changer. The maid I was able to hire has really spruced up the place."

"Okay, I'm not going to sit here and just let you yell at me."

"Great. Just run off again like you always do."

"I don't need this right now."

"Are you on drugs?"

Simon stopped and turned. "What? Are you crazy?"

"Then explain to me where you disappear to. Why have you completely checked out of our lives? I can't figure out if this has something to do with Mom or—"

"Don't you say it."

"Why? Why can't we talk about her? I know you cared about her, Simon."

"I've got to go."

"Why? What's so important? Just tell me what's going on with you!"

He removed his glasses and rubbed his eyes, as he usually did when he was stressed or uncomfortable. "Nothing you need to worry about."

"What is that supposed to mean? Is there something going on between you and Britney Kohl?"

"What? Why would you even say that?"

"She mentioned you. She sounded like a crazy person; said I was being watched. What is she talking about?"

Simon looked genuinely startled for a moment, but he quickly regained his composure and was on his way out again.

"Fine. Go. You always did take after Mom."

Simon stopped in the doorway. "Tell Dad I love him."

"Fuck you, Simon."

The door slammed. She waited until she heard his car drive away then buried her face in the cushions of the couch and screamed.

She had barely been asleep for an hour when she heard her dad calling her. She cursed, jumped out of bed, and ran to the opposite end of the trailer to her father's bedroom. She found him standing at the window, staring out into the night. "Dad? What is it? What are you doing out of bed? It's three in the morning."

"They're out there."

Hazy went to his side and attempted to gently steer him back to bed, but he wouldn't budge.

"They're out there," he said again.

Hazy looked out the window and couldn't see a thing except the woods they faced and the faint light of the trailer across the road from them.

"Dad, we've been over this a thousand times. The Francis kids are always out screwing around all hours of the night. I caught the youngest one trying to piss in our mailbox just two nights ago."

He continued staring straight ahead, unblinking. "No." He turned his face towards Hazy. "They were in the house."

Chills raced down Hazy's spine.

"What do you mean, Dad? Who?"

"Them. Always them."

"Okay, you're really starting to freak me out."

His mood suddenly shifted, and he began to weep. "I'm so sorry."

She wrapped her arms around him. She couldn't remember if she had ever seen him cry. Not even when Mom left. "It's okay, Dad."

"No…no, it's not," he said, sobbing.

"You're just tired. Simon kept you up too late. Between that and your new pills, your body's having a hard time adjusting." She took his hand and led him back to his bed. "You just need to rest, okay? You'll feel better in the morning."

She got him calm and tucked back in but didn't even make it to the door before he called to her again. His voice was slow and deep, containing none of the emotion from moments before.

"I've seen beyond the Veil."

"Okay, Dad. You are seriously freaking me out. What the hell was that?"

The only thing she heard in response was the sound of his snoring.

She slowly and quietly closed the door behind her and within seconds was frantically tearing through Simon's room, upending everything that wasn't nailed down, undeterred by the smell of unwashed clothes and festering trash. After one of Dad's medications had caused him to have a few volatile mood swings last year, Simon had thought it best to take away his gun and hide it. Hazy knew he had buried it away somewhere in his room, she just wasn't sure where. So far, the closet, bookcase, and desk drawers had all been a bust. She told herself she was probably overreacting. But everything that had happened in the past few hours had left her completely on edge. Paranoia and hallucinations aside, the fact was that there was indeed someone targeting teenage girls in Darlington Hills. At best they were tied up in a basement somewhere. At worst—well, she'd rather not think about it. No one had been reported missing since Nara, but the evil bastard was still out there roaming free. Hazy had never been more thankful for all the times her dad had taken her hunting when she was younger and forced her to get comfortable with handling a weapon. She just needed to find it.

She continued her search, clearing out the clutter beneath Simon's bed, but still nothing. She was starting to wonder if the gun was here after all. For all she knew, Simon had gotten rid of it completely. He always had been the squeamish one when it came to the idea of weapons and violence.

She stood up and rubbed her eyes, unsure of what to do next. The only place she hadn't checked was beneath the mattress. It seemed a little too obvious—that's where Dad had kept it in his room. It was likely the first place he would look if he came hunting for it. But for all his book smarts, Simon could be a little lacking in the common sense department.

She lifted the mattress as far as she could on the left-hand side, but nothing. When she lifted the right side, she had to do a double take. No gun, but something else. Lying face down was a small red book. She almost dismissed it as something private of Simon's and left it alone. There were some things she'd rather not know. But curiosity got the better of her. And there was something familiar about it…

She grabbed it, hesitantly turning the worn, stained cover over in her hands. The blood drained from her face.

Spelled out on the front cover, smudged but still visible, were the words *The Journal of Nara Kilday.*

CHAPTER 16

Hazy would be lucky to make it through the day alive. She'd already nearly fallen face first into boiling French fry grease, and she had just dropped her third tray of the day, slicing her hand open on a shattered drinking glass. If a random accident didn't end her, her boss or an angry customer would.

She was a wreck. Nerves shot, going on no sleep, with every ounce of mental energy devoted to playing and replaying last night's events in her head, trying to avoid coming to the worst possible conclusion—the one that she couldn't bring herself to accept—that her brother might somehow be involved with the disappearance of her best friend.

He had yet to respond to her dozens of phone calls and texts. She couldn't even begin to think about doing something drastic like going to the police until she heard from him, actually looked him in the eye, and let him explain himself. Simon hated violence. The idea of him hurting anyone was incomprehensible. There had to be another explanation. Had to be.

Most disturbing of all had been what Hazy had found in Nara's journal. Page after page of some of the most bizarre shit she had ever seen. Strange symbols. Disturbing messages. Crude diagrams. All written in what appeared to be dried blood. She could sooner accept her brother was a deranged psycho than Nara.

Nara, the girl who wouldn't even swear, who prayed before meals and volunteered at her church's food pantry. The girl who got visibly uncomfortable at the sight of a pentagram necklace. Hazy was supposed to believe that same girl had written all this. Had hidden it from her behind the world's most convincing church girl facade.

"You still in there, hon?" came the voice on the other side of the bathroom door. It was Marie, Hazy's fifty-something year old co-worker who liked to live vicariously through her. Marie had dated the same guy all through high school, then ended up divorced from him in her mid-forties. She felt she had wasted her best years with him and was now attempting to re-live her teenage years through Hazy. Hazy felt a little sorry for her, so she didn't mind too much. But today of all days she just wanted to be left the hell alone.

"Out in a minute!" Hazy called back. She finished washing the blood from her hands and applied an adhesive bandage over the cut. Thankfully, it hadn't been too deep. The last thing she needed was a hospital bill.

"Patrick wants to see you when you're done. I told him to go easy on you."

Great. A condescending lecture from her creep of a boss while he stared at her chest was just what she needed today. She had naively assumed she could set aside her life's unfolding nightmare and power through her shift. She couldn't afford not to. But one more screw up and she'd likely be out of job—if it wasn't too late already. She couldn't go on like this. She needed answers. Improvising, she wrapped her hand with an excessive amount of toilet paper and peeked out the bathroom door.

"How bad is it?" Marie asked, eyes full of concern.

Hazy help up her hand and put on her most pathetic face. "I think I'm going to need stitches."

"Oh, damn! I'm sorry, sweetie. What's going on with you? You don't seem yourself today. You know you can always talk to me."

"Just had a lot of shit going on at home. Nothing you need to worry about."

"Listen. Why don't you go get that looked at? I'll cover for you."

"What about Patrick? He'll be pissed."

"I'll handle Patrick, don't you even worry."

"Are you sure?"

"One hundred and ten percent."

"Thanks, Marie. I owe you!"

Hazy gave her a quick hug, raced out the back door, and instantly received due punishment for her deception.

There he stood. Stupid Elijah was standing over her car stuffing a note under the windshield wiper. For half a second, she considered turning around and going back inside but it was too late. He had already seen her, those pale blue eyes staring out from behind his mop of dark, messy hair.

"Oh. Hey."

"What the hell are you doing here?"

"Leaving you a note."

"I can see that. Why?"

"You have me blocked. You ignore me at school. I can't take it anymore."

Hazy grabbed the note and tore it in two. "What happened between us was a mistake, get it? We don't have anything to say to each other."

"No, *you* don't get it. She's all I can think about. I have nightmares, I can't sleep. Every time I close my eyes, I see her. Everyone thinks I had something to do with it. It's killing me, Hazy. I have nobody…"

She had never seen him like this. Never seen him display an ounce of emotion. All the times he had tried to reach out to her since Nara went missing, he had never seemed this…desperate.

She unlocked the car door and slid into the driver's seat. "Not my problem."

Elijah grabbed the door before she could shut it. "Please! Can we please just talk?"

"You think you're the only one who's suffering? We messed up, Elijah. We both failed her"—the pages of Nara's journal flashed in her mind—"and we both have to live with it."

By the look on his face, Hazy knew she had crushed him. But she didn't have it in her to be what he needed right now. She herself was drowning and no one was coming to save her, either.

She started the car and backed out of the parking lot into the street, tires screeching. In her rear-view mirror, Elijah remained where she had left him, standing still and alone.

CHAPTER 17

During her freshman year, Hazy had gone through a typical goth phase and done her fair share of lurking around graveyards and pretending to be really into death and the macabre. Even then, this place had given her the creeps. Pitch Black Books & Curiosities prided itself on specializing in the occult and obscure. It also happened to be Simon's favorite place in the whole world.

Behind the filthy, film-covered windows, stack after stack of old books completely obscured the interior. The painted wooden sign overhead was cracked and faded, and the building itself, sandwiched between a tattoo parlor and a vape shop, appeared to be perpetually on the verge of being condemned. Not the most inviting place, and the bum sleeping on the sidewalk didn't help. Hazy took a deep breath and put her car into park. Best to get this over with.

She carefully sidestepped the bum and took note of the odd address marker above the door—spelled out "Seven and One"—before stepping inside to the smell of incense, decaying paper, and something else she couldn't quite identify. Predictably, the store was dimly lit, with every visible nook and cranny stuffed floor to ceiling with books, candles, and unknown dead things in jars. Crystals and dream catchers hung from the ceiling, completing the look.

Hazy stepped up to the counter, which was occupied by a gaunt, freckled teenager with curly red hair who appeared to be completely absorbed by what she assumed to be some mystical old tome.

"Um, hi. I'm wondering if you've seen my brother lately? He hangs out here a lot. Simon Foss? Tall, dark hair, glasses."

He looked up from his book and closed it, revealing the front cover. Hazy stifled a laugh. *The Field Guide to Pokémon.* Mystical tome indeed.

"Huh?" he said, mouth drooping open.

It was clear she wasn't going to get far with this kid.

"Do you have a manager or someone I could talk to?"

"You must be Hazy."

She spun around.

The voice belonged to a woman who would have looked more at home with the PTA than at an occult bookstore. She was short, wide around the hips, and wearing an oversized hoodie with yoga pants, Frappuccino in one hand, phone in the other. The only thing remotely remarkable about her was her frizzy red hair, but even that had been reined in and loosely piled up into a bun.

"Sorry to sneak up on you. I'm Tessa. I sort of run the place." She looked past Hazy, raising her voice. "Derek! How many times have I told you to greet the customers when they walk in?" She turned back to Hazy. "Sorry. My sister's kid. You try to do someone a favor…." She smirked, shaking her head. "Anyway! As soon as I saw you come in, I knew it had to be you. Simon talks so much about you. How's he been?"

"I was actually hoping you could tell me. Has he been around lately?"

"No, not in a while. He's a good kid, though. Smart, observant. Always asking questions. Can I get you something to drink? Water? Coffee?"

Hazy was rarely afforded a look into Simon's life away from her. She wasn't thirsty, but she wanted to keep the woman talking, see if she could learn something.

"Water's fine, thanks."

Tessa turned and waved her hand. "Follow me."

She led Hazy through a veritable labyrinth of overflowing shelves, stuffed with volume after volume of dusty texts and forgotten manuscripts. They finally came to the end of a hallway where two doors faced each other. One was marked "Employees Only." The other, "Vault. Access Forbidden Except by Permission of Upper Management." Hazy rolled her eyes. These people took themselves way too seriously.

Tessa pulled out a ring of keys from her hoodie and unlocked the "Employees Only" door, motioning Hazy inside.

"Welcome to my office. Pardon the mess."

Hazy had half expected to find a dungeon or a crypt, but it was as surprisingly ordinary as Tessa herself. Sure, there were stacks of books and papers strewn about, and it could use a little ventilation, but it was your regular back-room office complete with desk, computer, and coffee maker.

"Have a seat!" Tessa said, nodding towards an empty chair in front of the desk. She bent down and pulled out a bottled water from a small refrigerator and handed it to Hazy. "Here you go. Should be cold. Put them in early this morning."

"Thanks. So, uh…how long have you worked here?"

Tessa plopped down into the chair behind her desk. The wall behind her was covered with framed black and white photos and pinned-up newspaper articles. Unsurprisingly, they all appeared to center around the paranormal—hauntings, UFO sightings, and witchery. Hazy's eye was drawn to old-timey painting at the center featuring a man in nineteenth-century clothing complete with handlebar mustache.

"Oh, about ten years or so. Started out like Derek, just manning the counter on weekends. But I guess the big boss saw something in me. Kept giving me more and more responsibilities until one day I was running the place. It's great, though. I get to be surrounded by what I love while my employer is freed up to be more active in the field."

"Cool. Well, I have to say, you don't really—"

"Look like I fit in here? Yeah, I get that a lot. But I love it. This is my world," she said, extending her arms out. "But I get the impression this is not really your thing. Not like your brother."

"No. No offense."

"It's okay. It's not for everyone. I have to ask, though. He's not in any trouble, is he?"

Hazy chose her words carefully.

"Things are just hectic at home, is all. I know he's got his own life. We had an argument last night. I'd really like the chance to clear the air. He's just not responding to me. I thought maybe I'd find him hiding out here."

"That sucks. Simon's told me a bit about your dad. How's he doing?"

How much had Simon divulged to this woman? And why had he never mentioned her?

"Oh, you know. Good days and bad days. Seems like mostly bad, though, lately."

"I'm sorry. Sounds like you're dealing with a lot." Tessa leaned forward to place her hand on Hazy's. Awkward. She barely knew her.

As her mind raced to contrive a way to excuse herself from the conversation, her eye was again drawn to the old painting hanging behind Tessa. In particular, she noticed a quote engraved in gold at the base of the frame. It read, "I've seen beyond the Veil. - William Darlington." Hazy had heard those words before....

She looked back to Tessa, who had begun to lightly caress Hazy's hand. "If there's anything I could do...."

Hazy abruptly pulled away and stood, accidentally knocking over a cup of ballpoint pens. "I'm sorry. I don't want to take any more of your time. Thank you for the water. Just...if you see Simon, could you tell him to call me?"

Tessa leaned back in her chair. "Of course."

Hazy turned to open the door.

"And it would be greatly appreciated if you could do the same. Unfortunately, Simon seems to have misplaced a certain book...a book that's very important to my employers. Doesn't look like much. Small thing with a bright red cover. One of a kind. You wouldn't have happened to have seen anything like that, would you?"

Hazy's heart pounded. She turned slowly back to face Tessa. The woman's entire demeanor had shifted, all traces of kindness and concern having vanished from her cold, green eyes. Tension swelled in the thick, stale air of the tight space as Hazy wondered just what the hell she had stumbled into.

At that moment, the door burst open. Hazy jumped back as a tall, bearded man covered in filthy, unmatched layers of clothing stumbled into the room, waving a knife ranting about not being able to use the restroom. He was the bum she had seen sleeping outside. Derek, red-faced and out of breath, followed right behind, his frantic pleas falling on deaf ears.

"Sir, sir. Please, sir! You can't go in there, sir!"

Tessa had backed herself in the far corner behind her desk, already dialing 911. Amid Derek's futile begging and Tessa's frantic call with dispatch, the man turned and locked eyes with Hazy. She was at once struck with relief and utter confusion. Beneath the dirt and grime, she recognized the face of the bum as Jack—the customer from her restaurant. He subtly nodded his head back towards the door. He was giving her an out. She didn't hesitate. She ran, weaving through the twisting maze of books until at last she burst out the front door into the welcoming light of the winter sun. Within seconds she was in her car, tires screeching as she backed out and sped off, never once looking back.

CHAPTER 18

The hallways reverberated with the sound of a thousand teenagers. Lockers creaked open and slammed shut, acting like the erratic beat to a chorus of gossip, shouts, and laughter. It was the music of a typical Monday morning at Darlington Hills High, and it was giving Hazy a splitting headache.

She was going on nearly forty-eight hours with no sleep, fueled by nothing but adrenaline, coffee, and paranoia. She paced back and forth in front of the stairwell, waiting for her opportunity to strike. Her target was a creature of habit and always took a restroom break between first and second period. While she waited, she fired off another text to Simon. She wasn't going to stop until he finally responded to her. She checked the time—only one minute until the next bell.

Finally, the target appeared, rounding the corner, miraculously alone. Hazy had heard that Britney had fallen out with Heather, but not even Violet was attached to her hip this morning. Perfect. Britney entered the girls' restroom alone, and Hazy made her move.

She shut the door behind her and scooted the trashcan over to act as a barricade. It probably wasn't enough to stop someone who really wanted in, but it would at least buy her a few seconds if she needed them. Britney, who had just begun fidgeting with her make-up, stopped, and looked away from the mirror.

"Hazy," she said nervously. "What's up?"

Hazy took three long strides, bringing her inches from Britney's face. "We need to talk."

Britney jumped back up against the slick, tiled wall.

"I have nothing to say to you," she said, staring into Hazy's bloodshot eyes.

Hazy inched closer. "What did you mean the other night, huh? Who's watching me? What's my brother got to do with this?"

"You're making me uncomfortable."

"Good!" Hazy slammed her hand into the wall next to Britney's head, causing her to flinch. "I know you had something to do with this. You hated Nara. Made her life hell! Did you set her up?"

"Yes, I hated her!" Britney fired back. "When I was a kid…her cop dad sent my dad to prison over a bullshit drug charge. He ruined my family. I wanted her to suffer." Her eyes welled up with tears. "But I swear…"

"What did you do?"

Britney put her head in her hands as tears streamed down her cheeks. "I swear, I didn't know what they were planning."

Hazy jumped at the sound the sound of metal screeching against tile. Someone was trying to push through the door.

Her hands began to shake. "What happened?" she said through gritted teeth.

Britney collapsed to the floor sobbing, her words coming out in stuttered inhalation. "I—I don't know…I didn't—it was just supposed to be…to be fun…like a party…at the circle in the woods. I didn't think they were serious—that…that they would actually…hurt anybody."

The intruder banged on the door. Hazy knelt down and grabbed Britney by her collar. "Who?! I need to know—was Nara there? Did they hurt her?"

"I…saw her…but I don't know. I don't…I can't…"

The banging got louder. The trashcan screeched. They were almost through.

"Spit it out!"

"I can't…I can't…"

The door burst open sending the metal trashcan crashing to the hard tiled floor with an ear-splitting clang. Hazy quickly stood and turned to see raven haired, goth princess Violet.

"What did you do to her, Foss?"

Hazy looked down at Britney, who had seemed to suddenly regain control of herself.

Violet turned her head and called out "Mister Dargo!"

Hazy stormed towards the door, shoving her aside. "Out of my way, bitch."

CHAPTER 19

Elijah opened the front door and stared, expression blank.

"Did you get my text?" Hazy asked impatiently.

Elijah ran a hand through his shaggy, unkempt hair.

"Yeah. Thought you didn't want anything to do with me."

"Will you just shut up and let me in? This is important. And it's freaking cold out here."

He stood to the side.

"Thank you." She entered the apartment to the smell of coffee and cigarettes. Elijah's dad was passed out in his recliner, snoring, while the TV blared some ad for prescription medication. She followed Elijah to his room. He promptly shut the door behind them, plopped down on his unmade bed, picked up his guitar, and began strumming. Hazy shoved a pile of dirty clothes off his desk chair and sat down.

She scanned the walls of his bedroom, cluttered with punk and death metal posters and the occasional tattoo model. There was a small space dedicated to Xeroxed flyers from all of his band's gigs. Curiously missing was the one from the night of their indiscretion. An image flashed in her mind. Them, in the back of his van, in the heat of the moment. She quickly pushed it away.

"So, is this what you do all day? Sit here and feel sorry for yourself?"

"Fuck you, Hazy. You have no idea what I've gone through."

She hated to admit it to herself, but he was right. Her life had been shit, but Elijah had been tagged as a suspect almost immediately after Nara went missing. Sheriff Kilday had been especially hard on him. Elijah's rocky relationship with Nara hadn't been a secret to anyone. Of course, Elijah's choice of music and friends didn't help matters either. He had endured numerous police questionings and had his name blasted across the news and social media.

"Look, I'm sorry. But we really need to talk. There's some crazy shit going down, and I don't have anyone else to turn to."

Elijah looked up and glared.

"I know, I know. I was a total bitch to you. And you have every right to tell me to piss off. But this…what I've seen concerns both of us. It could help clear your name. Even if it does risk ruining mine."

He looked down and continued strumming.

"Here. Just look at this." Hazy reached into her backpack and pulled Nara's journal. He stopped and looked up.

"What is it?"

"Just look at it. Please."

Elijah took the journal and began to thumb through it. His face remained expressionless.

Hazy grew impatient at his lack of reaction. "Well? What do you think? Isn't that seriously jacked up?"

"I don't get it."

Hazy grabbed the journal from him, opened to a random page, and pointed. "This! Look at this shit! It's not normal." Elijah shrugged. "Nara drew stuff like that all the time. So what?"

"What do you mean?"

He sat his guitar aside, reached under his bed, and pulled out an old, beat up cigar box covered in stickers. "This is pretty much the only thing the police didn't get when they ransacked the place. Luckily, I had left it behind in Bryan's garage after our last practice."

He pulled back the lid, revealing a collection of paper scraps, sheets ripped from spirals, even the backs of napkins. "These are all the lyrics Nara ever wrote for me."

Hazy gazed at them hesitantly.

"Go ahead. Check 'em out. I got nothing to hide."

She grabbed the sheet at the top, unfolding it. Filling the margins around the handwritten lyrics were doodles that looked unmistakably like the writing in the journal. Hazy grabbed another piece of paper, then another, and another. Some pages had more than others, but most, if not all, had a least a couple of the symbols scrawled somewhere along the edges.

"Surprise. Nara had a dark side. Have you never read her lyrics?"

Hazy was struck by shame and a dash of jealousy. Had Nara hidden a side of herself from Hazy? Or had Hazy just refused to see it? Had she been just as guilty as everyone else of painting Nara as a one-dimensional goody-goody?

"I asked her about the doodles a couple times, but she would get weirded out by it. Acted like she didn't even remember writing them. I figured she was embarrassed so I just left it alone. But man, could she write some heavy shit. Don't know how she did it. She always seemed so…good, you know. Like a really good person, I mean. I don't know how this stuff came out of her."

Elijah went quiet as his eyes drifted towards the ceiling. He seemed to be somewhere else. "I never felt good enough for her. Maybe that's why I was always screwing up. I knew I didn't deserve her."

While Nara had become an enigma to Hazy, Elijah was starting to make a lot more sense. She continued thumbing through the stack of lyrics. She picked one at random and began to read.

Child of shadow. Child of sin.

Choking back light, it dies within

I surrender all to Inferno's spell

Child of shadow. Child of Hell.

I hide my face from Heaven's flame

Keep me close, forget my name

I raise a glass to toast my fall

Bow to regret at curtain's call.

Hazy could hardly believe what she was reading. She swallowed. "Are they all like this?"

Elijah thumbed through the journal. "No. She wrote a lot of basic stuff. About love and break-ups and whatever. But most of 'em? Yeah." He reached into his back pocket for his wallet and removed a folded piece of paper. "This was the last one she wrote for me. Right before everything happened. I keep it on me…well, I don't really know why. It's like a piece of her for me to hold on to, I guess. And I don't know. This one felt…different."

It crinkled as Hazy unfolded it. The paper was warped and much of the ink was smeared or blurred. "Did you get this wet?"

"No. She gave it to me like that. I think…I think maybe it's from her tears. I'm telling you, it's different. I think Nara knew something bad was going to happen."

Hazy read.

Shadespawn, they call me, conceived
under a blood-soaked moon.

Angels cried and devils danced as I
quickened in my mother's womb

Through fire and water and
shattered earth

God hid his eyes at my cursed birth

Now Death has come to claim its prize

A sinner's blade grants my demise

By wounded stone behold, the path of threefold scars

In a shallow grave I'll stir, under fallen shining star

By rings of salt speak holy verse

Sinner's blood to break the curse

I've seen beyond the Veil.

I pray to no avail.

Hazy slumped back in her chair, disturbed. "What the hell?"

"Exactly."

For several moments, neither spoke. All was quiet save the muffled sounds of the TV in the other room.

"This phrase, 'I've seen beyond the Veil.' This may sound crazy, but it keeps popping up. My dad said it the other night. I thought it was just the medication talking. Then the next day I saw it on an old portrait at Pitch Black."

"Pitch Black? What were you doing there?"

"Never mind that right now. The portrait was of William Darlington."

"The dude that started the town. Yeah, I know. He's famous for that quote."

"Wait...he is? You know about this?"

"Yeah, a band called Demonocracy wrote a whole song about him." Elijah pulled a vinyl LP from his shelf. On the cover was a painted, hellish landscape beneath jagged indecipherable letters, presumably the band's logo. Elijah removed the lyric sheet and pointed to a song called "Witch Hammer."

"The song talks about how Darlington went crazy after his daughter disappeared and got all obsessed with all the weird shit he'd discovered. He blamed it all on witchcraft. He believed there was some old coven of witches hiding out in the woods."

"Mister Dargo left that out of his history lesson," Hazy said, scanning the lyrics, some of which seemed tame compared to what she had just seen from Nara. There it was, in the chorus. *I've seen beyond the Veil.* "Is it possible Nara heard this song when she was around you and it just got stuck in her head?"

"Don't think so. She hated death metal. Never let me play it when she was around."

Suddenly something jumped out at Hazy. "This part here: '*Seven and One/The devil runs free/Seven and One/ Kill another for me.*' Pitch Black's address is spelled out 'seven and one.' What does it mean?"

"Lots of pagans and Satanists use it. It's a reference to God resting on the seventh day in Genesis. Seven plus one is eight—the eighth day. The devil's day. God sleeps while the devil runs free. Sometimes it's just written as seventy-one. Or seventeen."

"Seventeen. Nara was seventeen. So were Becca and Melani. You don't think that—"

"Don't go there, Hazy."

"What? It's been three months. Everyone wants to avoid the obvious…that they're all probably dead."

"No, I don't believe that. She has to be alive. She has to be."

"Is that what you really believe? Or do you need it to be true to assuage your conscience? You'd feel guilty if she died after what we did, knowing she died hating you. Hating both of us."

Elijah slumped back down onto his bed. He picked up Nara's journal again, running his hand across the cover. "So, what are you saying? Do you really think there's some kind of satanic conspiracy behind it all?"

Hazy adjusted her headband. "I don't know what to think. But there's too much weird shit going on. It's all adding up to something."

"Why haven't you gone to your brother with all this? He's smart. Isn't he into all that paranormal conspiracy stuff?"

"You can't tell anyone, you hear me?"

"What?"

"Simon…he may be involved somehow. He's been avoiding me. And…" She took the journal from Elijah and held it up. "I found this hidden in his room."

"No shit?"

"Promise me, Elijah. This stays between us. If he… if he really knows something, or did something, I will turn him in myself. But I've got to know for sure first." She handed the journal back to him. "But I need you to keep this safe for me. No one can know you have it."

"Okay. What are you going to do?"

Hazy stood and again examined the pages of song lyrics. "I think Nara was out in the woods, at the circle. Whatever happened, happened out there. And maybe...maybe she's still out there. I have to find her."

She laid all the pages out on Elijah's floor, snapping pictures of each one.

"What are you doing?"

"Just covering my bases. I have pictures of every page of the journal too." She finished, gathered them all up again, and returned them to the cigar box. She handed it back to Elijah. "Thank you. For everything. I'm sorry for...for the things I said. I..." They locked eyes, and for a moment she found herself drawn to those baby blues of his, recalling the night of her weakness and betrayal. Hazy quickly caught herself and turned away before the thought could give birth to further temptation. "I've got to go."

She threw her backpack over her shoulder and opened the bedroom door.

"Let me walk you out," Elijah said, following right behind.

They passed Elijah's dad, still slumbering in the glow of the TV. They were almost to the front door when something on the screen caught Hazy's eye. She stopped cold.

"Wait. Turn it up!"

A breaking news story played out on the screen, with a video surveillance image of the man she knew as Jack, just as he had appeared at Pitch Black. Elijah retrieved the remote from the recesses of his father's recliner cushions.

"...believed to be a person of interest in the case of the three missing teenage girls. Former FBI agent Noel Raddemer is wanted in connection to multiple counts of criminal activity over the past few years after having quit the Bureau under mysterious circumstances. Raddemer is considered armed and dangerous. If you have any information regarding his current whereabouts, please contact Darlington Hills police or the FBI."

Hazy stood stunned. "Holy shit."

"What? You know him?"

"If they have that footage, they know I was there. They'll probably be looking for me," Hazy muttered to herself. She turned to Elijah, eyes wide. "I've got to go now!" She turned and threw open the front door and raced down the stairs in three quick strides.

"Hazy, wait!"

"Check on my dad for me! I'll text you!" She yelled from her car window as she sped out of the apartment parking lot.

CHAPTER 20

The hike through Veilwood had been long, exhausting, and at times treacherous. After several cuts, bruises, and one nasty rip in the sleeve of her favorite jacket, Hazy had finally reached her destination—the ancient monument of stones deep within the heart of the forest. The trek had taken her much longer than she anticipated, and now daylight was waning. Before approaching the circle, she looked back over her shoulder into the darkening thicket for probably the thousandth time. She was tired, on edge, and jumping at every creaking branch and rustling leaf. A couple of times she had even been convinced she glimpsed glowing lights flickering through the trees. She chalked it up to sleep deprivation and her rising sense of paranoia. Regardless of the danger, real or imagined, she wouldn't turn back. She owed it to Nara to uncover the truth, wherever it might lead.

Alone, in the deepening shadows of twilight, the six towering stones appeared more ominous and intimidating than she remembered them. Jutting up from the forest floor, each ranging between eight and ten feet tall, there was a presence to them that she had either denied or been ignorant to before. But perhaps most chilling—each of the stones were now split by a large crack running top to bottom. Even the seventh stone, horizontally positioned at the center—the one Simon had referred to as an altar—lay cleaved in two.

Hazy crossed the circle and approached the particular stone Nara had touched before blacking out. She reached out, placing her own hand on its cold, coarse surface, tracing the grooves of the engraved markings with her fingers. But she experienced no sacred vision or supernatural rebuke. If there were answers to be found here, it wouldn't be by divine intervention.

She removed her phone from her backpack and began scrolling through her photo roll, comparing the images from Nara's journal and Elijah's lyrics to the stone hieroglyphs. The similarities were striking. Age, weather, and the recent cracking may have obscured them to an extent, but there was no mistaking the resemblances in style and characteristics—the same sharp angles mixed with wild curves and crisscrossing lines. Soon she made an exact match, and then another and another. Nara had even produced what looked to be a crude pronunciation key next to her depictions, but when Hazy attempted to put it together, it just came out as nothing more than gibberish. If it was meant to be a real language, it didn't sound like anything she recognized.

A sudden blast of cold, howling wind swept through the circle. Trees rattled and leaves scattered. Hazy shivered and raised the collar of her jacket. She questioned the wisdom of staying out here much longer. Daylight was fading and darkened clouds were creeping in, but she wasn't ready to turn back. Not yet.

She traversed the perimeter of the circle, kicking over rocks and brush, futilely searching for some clue to what had happened out here. It had been months. If something nefarious had taken place, chances were the perpetrator, or nature itself, had long since erased any evidence. This was of course assuming that Britney had been telling the truth. The girl may have been petty and vindictive, but Hazy couldn't dismiss the terror she had heard in her voice. She believed her.

Frustrated, she sat down on the edge of the broken altar. She didn't know where to go from here. She had hoped against hope for some clue or lead to point the way. But she was starting to realize she was in way over her head. What did she know about crime scenes, or monuments, or weird ancient writing? She didn't want to have to go to the police. She had lost Nara and her mom while her dad continued to deteriorate. She couldn't bear the thought of losing Simon too. He was all she had left. But he wasn't leaving her much of a choice. She didn't know whether to cry or scream.

She swiped open her phone again, once more searching the photos for something she may have missed. There were many more bizarre things Nara had drawn besides the symbols—sketches, drawings, diagrams. She had never known Nara to be much of an artist, but then, she was discovering lots of things she never knew about her best friend.

Which brought her to Nara's lyrics. She pored through them again, this time stopping to focus solely on the words. Beneath the dark and violent prose, she found them to be both haunting and sad. The final one she wrote, according to Elijah, stuck with her the most. It almost read like a parting message. Like Elijah said…like she knew something bad was going to happen.

Now Death has come to claim its prize

A sinner's blade grants my demise

By wounded stone behold, the path of threefold scars

In a shallow grave I'll stir, under fallen shining star

The words jumped out at her. She looked down upon the split stone on which she sat, its other half lying flat on the forest floor, its sharp and angled end almost pointing like an arrow, past the circle, into the woods.

By wounded stone behold....

Could it be?

The sun had dipped below the horizon and the moon hung full in the overcast sky. She stood, activating her phone's flashlight, and walked in a straight line using the stone as her compass. She crossed out of the circle into the wild dark of the forest, where keeping straight became increasingly difficult. She repeated the words in her head—*behold the path of threefold scars*. If there was anything to this—if she hadn't gone completely insane—then there should be something to mark her way. The idea of a path in the thick brush seemed ridiculous. She scanned ahead with her flashlight—but there was nothing but trees. Endless trees.

Wait. What was that? She marched forward, pushing her way through choking bramble and jagged limbs, keep her light and focus directly ahead. The tree was thin, upright, smooth, and completely unremarkable—save for the symbol carved into its trunk. She couldn't believe it.

She snapped a photo and pressed on, going deeper and farther into darkness, so fixated on her goal that she barely took note of the drop in temperature or the distant roll of thunder. Then, there it was—the second marked tree. She snapped another photo and continued, slowly descending with the plunging and increasingly precarious terrain.

Finally, she found it. The third tree. Lightning flashed and the wind howled.

...threefold scars.

Hazy felt her stomach drop as her thoughts turned to the next line.

In a shallow grave I'll stir, under fallen shining star.

She swept the immediate area with her flashlight. No sooner was she contemplating the significance of "fallen shining star" did she catch a reflective glint in the light. *No. Please, God. No.*

For a moment, the world around her faded as the impossible and inevitable collided. Tangled in the branches of a sapling sycamore hung Nara's necklace, the one Hazy had given her on her seventeenth birthday. A jagged break ran through the center of the five-pointed star, its luster lost to the elements.

Hazy went to her knees, frantically clearing away the leaves and foliage surrounding the tree. She clawed away inches of wet dirt as her eyes welled with tears. The gray, lifeless flesh of a human hand lay just beneath the surface.

Hazy fell on her face and wept bitterly into the cold, indifferent earth. Rain began to fall.

CHAPTER 21

"Hazy. Hazy. Wake up!"

"Simon?" she muttered, slowly emerging from her deep slumber. "I had the craziest dream…" she said, her voice dry and cracked. She was cold. So cold.

"You need to get up, get your blood flowing."

Not Simon. She didn't recognize the voice. *Where am I?*

"You don't want to catch hypothermia."

"Huh…? What?"

Thunder cracked overhead. She bolted up from the dirt, wet and gasping from the cold. Reality came crashing down around her. She hadn't been dreaming. She was living a nightmare. She wiped her eyes and saw a face staring back at her from the dark, illuminated by the glow of a flashlight. She jumped back, scrambling through the mud to put distance between her and the stranger.

"Didn't mean to frighten you. I don't think we've had a proper introduction. I'm Noel," he said, pulling back the hood of his raincoat.

Recognition dawned on her. But there was something different about him.

"I know who you are. You're wanted by the police. Is that why you shaved your beard?"

He rubbed his face. "It was too bad. I was really starting to like it. But to put your mind at ease, the police don't have a clue what they're dealing with. They've got the wrong guy."

"I'm not so sure. You've apparently been stalking *me.*"

"Fair point. Can I give you dry jacket? You've got to be freezing. I've got one in my pack."

The rain had eased into a light drizzle, but she was soaked and shivering. She wanted so badly to say yes. "Depends."

"No strings attached. I just want to help." He removed his large hiking pack and sat it on the ground. Besides being loaded up with a bedroll, cooking pot, and canteen, she noted a hefty axe strapped to its side. Noel unzipped the pack and produced a weathered brown jacket about two sizes too big for her.

"Stay where you are," she said, arm extended in caution. "Just throw it."

She caught it, put it up to her nose, and gave it a quick sniff.

"It's clean," he said. "I'm honestly pretty normal, you know, outside of living in the woods and occasionally disguising myself as a bum to rescue innocent girls from nefarious bookstore owners."

Hazy enveloped herself in the jacket, pulling snug around her body. "Was that supposed to be funny?"

"I don't know. Look, I just—"

"Just tell me what the hell you want, okay? I'm cold, I'm tired, and I just found…" Hazy thought she might be sick. She looked down at the final resting place of her best friend, situated between her and Noel, and choked back tears. She wasn't about to cry in front of this stranger.

"I'm really sorry. But you've done good, Hazy. Now, you just need to finish what you started."

"Just what exactly do you mean by that?

"*By wounded stone behold, the path of threefold scars. In a shallow grave I'll stir, under fallen shining star,*'" he chanted.

"How do you know that?"

He looked away for a moment, his face pensive. "It's a long story. But you did it. You found her. Now you need to free her."

"What do you mean by that?"

"The rest of the words. '*In sacred rings speak holy verse. Sinner's blood to break the curse.*' You may not have noticed. Look around you."

Noel waved his flashlight across the ground. Surrounding them, at a diameter of about twenty-five feet, was a circle of white.

"Is that—"

"Salt. It provides a certain level of protection. But it's only temporary. These woods are cursed. Evil thrives here and has for a very long time. There is safer ground a little bit farther out. I have shelter there. But we can't move until we finish here."

Hazy put her head in her hands and tugged at her hair. "I'm sorry...this is all—"

"Crazy? Sure. But I can't deny what I've seen. You can't either."

"I don't know what I've seen! For all I know the killer wrote those words and passed them off as Nara's. Maybe you did! I sure as hell don't know what your interest in all this is. We should be going to the police!"

Noel went down on one knee and placed his hand upon the dirt. "A long time ago I made a promise. And I've come back to honor it. But I need your help."

She threw up her hands in exasperation. "Why? Why me?"

"Sinner's blood to break the curse."

"What's that supposed to mean? I'm not perfect so you get to label me a sinner? You don't know the first thing about me, buddy. All you supposedly morally upright people always passing judgment like you're better than everyone else."

"That's not really fair, is it? Did Nara ever treat you that way?"

A lump formed in her throat. What right did he have to invoke her name? She wanted to curse, to scream, to spit in his face. He had no right…

"Now, if you're done, I can explain. That's not what it means at all. Sinner, I believe, refers to Nara's killer. Sinner's blood, as in blood relation. You. Only you can break the curse because your brother murdered Nara."

"No…No! Don't you dare!"

"You know it's true, Hazy. It's why you didn't go to the police with Nara's journal. You're afraid. I don't blame you. But your brother has gone down a very dark path."

She couldn't hold back any longer. Tears streamed down her face.

"You stay the hell away from me."

She turned and ran.

CHAPTER 22

Reckless and aimless, Hazy ran and kept running—from Noel, from Nara, from everything. She didn't care if she ended up lost and alone or freezing to death at the bottom of a ravine. She just needed to get away—far away. She flew blindly through the dark, crashing through limb and brush until—*Wham!* She was flung backwards, slamming hard into the mud.

She rolled over and spat out dirt, trying to catch her breath. Whatever she had collided with appeared to have already recovered and was crawling back to its feet. To her left and right, lights appeared, casting a flickering orange glow. She looked up as a face came into focus.

"Hello, sis," Simon said, reaching out his hand to help her up. His face was pale and lined with sweat.

She refused his hand and instead rose to her feet using a tree trunk as leverage. She remained hunched over, still gasping for breath. She looked past Simon to his right and his left, to the source of the lights. Four individuals stood bearing torches, faces hidden, each completely cloaked in black.

"What the hell, Simon? Seriously…?"

"Do you have it?" His voice was stern and devoid of emotion.

"You ignore my every text and call and that's all you have to say to me?"

He rubbed his eyes beneath his glasses. "Don't be difficult. Just tell me where it is. I know you found it."

"Are you kidding me with this shit? Are you in a fucking cult?"

Simon lunged forward and grabbed her by the arm of her jacket. "I'm not playing around, Hazy! Where's the journal?"

"Let go of me!"

She thrashed her arms, trying to break free of his grip. He squeezed tighter. With all the strength she had left, she reared back and slapped him across the face, knocking his glasses off. He released his hold and stumbled back, clutching his cheek. The four cloaked cultists edged closer. Simon held out his hand, signaling them to halt.

He looked back to Hazy, his eyes a mix of fury and fear. "You've made a big mistake."

"What did you do, Simon? Did you kill those girls? Did you kill Nara?!"

He reached down to pick up his glasses. "Everything I've done," he said, his voice shaking, "I did for my family. For us!"

Hazy closed her hand over her mouth. She stepped back, her eyes wet with tears. "Oh my God. Oh my God!"

"I tried doing this the easy way. Search her backpack."

The cultists began to move forward when a voice called from the dark. "Don't lay a hand on her."

Noel stepped into the light.

"You. I should have known you'd be skulking about."

"Let her go, Simon. You don't want to do this."

Simon reached into his jacket, pulled out a revolver and aimed it at Noel.

Hazy screamed. "What are you doing?"

He cocked the gun. "Your new friend here...did he tell you how Nara's body ended up in that grave? Did he tell you how he put her there, trying to enact some kind of ritual? You can't trust him, Hazy."

At that moment, the forest was lit up by a blinding strike of lightning, followed by a seismic clap of thunder. Noel acted swiftly and slammed into Simon, knocking the gun from his hand. It tumbled away, landing inches from Hazy's feet.

"Hazy, run!" shouted Noel before delivering a well-placed punch to Simon's jaw.

Two of the cultists closed in on Noel while the other two advanced towards Hazy. She quickly reached for the gun, pulled it from the mud, and ran, dodging and weaving through the forest with the cultists in close pursuit. By the sound of their grunting and heavy breathing, too close. They were bigger, faster, and about to overtake her. She slipped out of the straps of her backpack and tossed it aside, hoping it would divert them. One turned to go after it, but the other stayed on her. She gripped the handle of the revolver, hoping she remembered everything her dad had taught her.

She felt a hand grab her shoulder and the next thing she knew her face slammed into the dirt with the weight of two hundred pounds on her back. The man in the cloak turned her over, but she was ready for him. She pointed the revolver at his gut and pulled the trigger.

Click.

She cocked and fired again.

Click. Click. Click.

Damn it, Simon!

The man laughed then slapped the gun out of her hands. He pressed down upon her with his full weight and wrapped his hands around her neck, squeezing. Hazy kicked and hit and thrashed. His face hovered over hers, still hidden by the hood of his cloak, his breath hot and rancid. Hazy reached out with her hands, feeling for a rock, a stick, anything. Then the impossible happened. The man's eyes began to glow, pure white with a faint halo of green, completely devoid of pupils. Hazy tried to scream, but it came out as a ragged gurgle. The man—or whatever the hell he was—opened his mouth wide with a sound like strained inhalation. The edges of her vision began to darken, and she felt suddenly weak, like the life was draining from her.

She heard the sound of a dull thud and then felt his hands release her neck and his weight lift from her body. Her vision fully returned to see Noel standing above her, holding a heavy, gnarled tree branch.

"Get up! Get back to the cir—"

The second cultist had returned, sideswiping Noel. They went down hard, brawling furiously in the dark. Hazy didn't hesitate to make her escape, but her body reeled. She stumbled forward, pushing as fast as her feet would carry her. She could see a light just ahead breaking through the trees.

Thunder boomed and rain began to pour again. She picked up speed as her strength returned, sprinting towards the light. She could see it clearly now—a beam rising up from the earth. Noel had left his flashlight behind staked into the ground to light the way back. Hazy crossed the supposed protective ring of salt and collapsed onto the ground next to Noel's pack. She pulled her phone from her pocket, trying to keep it shielded from the rain with her jacket, and dialed 911. No signal. She tried again and again, to no avail. *Damn it!*

Something growled in the dark. She looked up to see two cultists emerge from the shadows, soon followed by another. Their hoods were drawn now—two men and a woman. Their eyes glowed. Hazy reached for Noel's pack and unstrapped the axe. She stood, gripping it tight with both hands, holding it at the ready.

"Come on, you assholes! Just try it!"

They paced back and forth around the circle like caged animals, hissing and snarling. As impossible as it seemed, they wouldn't cross the barrier. She couldn't believe it. It seemed the last several hours were proving to be a serious challenge to her perception of reality.

With the downpour showing no signs of ceasing, she questioned how well the integrity of the ring would hold. Another dial to 911 proved futile, and her battery was nearly dead. Hazy was trapped, drenched, freezing, and running out of options. She sat down in the pooling water and leaned back up against the small sycamore. She wasn't sure God existed, but she looked up to the heavens and called out nonetheless.

"Come on, please! Can I catch a freakin' break here?!"

Just above her and slightly over to left, something swayed in the torrential rain. Nara's necklace still hung from the tree. The words repeated in her head, "*Under shining silver star.*"

It was totally insane, but what did she have to lose at this point? She removed her jacket and lifted it over head for the little shelter it would provide while she re-read the lyrics. What holy words? And what curse was she supposed to break? Nara's remains were buried beneath her feet under inches of dirt and water. She was dead. There was nothing she could do to change that.

The savage cultists continued their frenzied pacing. They appeared to be getting braver, testing the limits of the circle as the hammering rain began to dilute the barrier. Hazy pulled the axe close, tightening her grip.

"Hazy!"

Simon appeared at the edge of the circle, bleeding from a wound on his forehead. Noel was with him. Simon pushed him to his knees, placing his recovered revolver to Noel's temple.

"I'm not going to ask again. Where is it?!" he shouted above the deluge.

Hazy stood defiant, axe in hand. "I know it's not loaded."

Simon reached into his inner jacket pocket and produced a single bullet. He loaded the weapon and placed it back to Noel's head.

"You were saying?"

"I don't have it, Simon! You can't do this! This is not you!"

"You don't know anything about me."

"Finish it, Hazy! Speak the words!" Noel yelled above the downpour.

Simon cocked the gun.

"What words? This is crazy! I don't know what the hell I'm supposed to do!"

"The trees!" Noel shouted before Simon whipped him with the butt of his pistol. He collapsed unconscious into the wet soil.

"The trees? The trees..." Hazy muttered to herself.

Several more cultists appeared out of the dark and surrounded the edge of the ring. Panicked, Hazy looked back to her phone, swiping to the photos she had taken of the marked trees that led her to the ring. Three symbols.

The cultists began to chant.

She scrolled back to the pages of Nara's phonetic pronunciations, hastily scanning for the matching symbols in a desperate race against her phone's dying battery.

Simon called out as the chanting grew louder. "What are you doing with your phone? Hazy?" Realization suddenly dawned on him. "Oh, of course. Smart. Very smart. So where is it? Where did you hide it? You may as well tell me. Because when this barrier breaks, I won't be able to stop them from coming in there and taking the phone from you. We'll get what we need either way. But my boss is old fashioned. Prefers the touch of the real thing in his hands."

Hazy remained focused, drowning out Simon's chatter and the incessant chanting. Bam! She found the first match. Setting aside all sense of dignity, reason, and rationality, she spoke it aloud. "*Ta!*"

"Whatever you think you're doing, it's not going to work. I need that journal, Hazy. Where did you hide it?"

Hazy located the second match. "*Koom!*"

The cultists all took a step forward as the circle of salt began to dissolve against the persistence of the flood. Hazy scrolled and scrolled, checking each symbol against the final mark from the trees.

The chanting grew louder. The rain surged and thunder clashed. Simon screamed again, "Hazy!"

"Got it." She looked up and spoke, "*Leetha!*"

The chanting stopped. Simon looked around nervously. Hazy had no idea what the hell she had just done, but she had expected something—anything—to happen. Nothing did. The chanting resumed as the cult advanced against the weakening barrier.

Maybe she had them in the wrong order? She went to her phone to recheck her work and watched the screen turn black. That was it.

Shit!

She tried another combination. "Um...*Koom Leetha Ta!*"

"Hazy! They are coming through. I can't stop them unless you give me something!"

"*Leetha Ta Koom!*"

"Hazy!"

The barrier broke. The cult surged forward.

Hazy shattered her phone against the tree and fell to her knees. She placed her hands on Nara's sodden, shallow grave, and closed her eyes.

"TALEETHAKOOM!"

The light died.

The rain stopped.

And a chorus of inhuman shrieks pierced the night.

CHAPTER 23

The girl dwelt in darkness. Beyond the Veil, hope and light were anathema. Amid a grotesque assembly of the forsaken and fallen, she abided.

Here, beyond the Veil, denizens fed on despair and gave birth to malevolence. It repulsed her. And it beckoned her.

But above the infernal clamor of unclean spirits, a summons went forth, uttered in meager and evanescent faith, echoing backwards and forwards in time.

"Little girl, arise."

Familiar words, both ordinary and sacred, rattled idle bones.

"Little girl, arise."

Words, simple yet significant, stirred scattered blood.

"Little girl, arise."

Words both calm and insurgent forged flesh anew.

The Veil was torn.

A cold presence observed from the shadows and raged.

The girl quickened within her miry womb of earth and water. Writhing, grasping, clawing, she ascended from the sludge. With a great heave she breached the surface and convulsed at the sudden intake of air and the expulsion of muck from her lungs.

Evil converged.

Resting before her, as if awaiting a call to action, lay a harsh, gleaming blade. The girl took it in her hands, ascended, and began to fight.

CHAPTER 24

Hazy's world had gone black. She knew nothing but damp and bitter cold. Her strength was gone, and she had lost all feeling in her limbs. Rough hands had swept her up, carried her for some distance, then dumped her like a sack of potatoes. She hadn't moved since. Couldn't. She was done. Had given all she could. Against all sound judgment she had entertained the possibilities of magic and miracles. If there had been some secret to unlock, some reversal of Nara's fate, she had failed. Her reward would be a cold, insignificant death, alone and far from home. At this point, she welcomed it. But death was slow in coming.

Muffled voices rose and fell. The conversation was heated, with apparently some disagreement on exactly what to do with her. It seemed Simon had done something to upset his new masters. *Good. He can go to Hell.*

The dispute escalated. First there was shouting, then things got physical. Sounds of hitting, shoving…cracking? Full-throated screaming. She sensed the vibration of running feet. Hands clutched her upper arms, attempting to rouse her from her frigid catatonic state.

"Hazy! Hazy! Get up!"

It sounded like Simon. His hands gripped tighter, and he shook her violently. She may have mumbled a curse under her breath. When she finally managed to crack an eyelid, she was met with a cloudy image her brother's terror-stricken face. Behind him was nothing but blurred chaos.

"Wake up, damn it!"

He stopped shaking and instead began to pull, dragging her through the thick, rain-soaked slush. The screaming and shouting continued all around her. Her eyes flickered open to witness a moonlit scene of absolute horror. Bodies running. Limbs flying. Blood spraying. Something moved among the glowy-eyed cultists, chopping and hacking with brutal grace and precision. Divine judgment had arrived by the blade of an axe, but was its wielder angel or demon?

The remaining cultists regrouped and formed up in a circle surrounding the assassin, giving Hazy her first clear view. Filthy, tattered clothes hung from the tall, slender frame of the axe-bearer. She slowly turned towards Hazy, her blood and mud splattered face radiant in light of the moon. Her hair was shorter, her eyes now fierce and defiant, but there was no mistaking the girl she had once called her best friend.

Nara stood before her, a living vision of terror and savage beauty. That's when Hazy was certain. With a cold induced hallucination, death had come to claim her.

The girl locked eyes with the stranger. She knew that face. Had known. It triggered a confusing amalgam of emotions. There was bitter enmity, but also deep affection. She watched as the stranger fell into unconsciousness and was then carried away into the night by another. That one provoked something else, something more visceral. In his eyes she saw death.

She leaned over and removed the axe from the chest of the fallen enemy at her feet, then gauged her situation. They had her surrounded—the three who remained that hadn't fled or fallen by her blade. They looked like men, save for the greenish glow of their eyes and the rage of their minds. She could see through the Veil, could see that they had given themselves over to restless and corrupting spirits.

They came for her, but the girl was ready. Propelled by instinct, she weaved and flowed, evading the reach of their arms and swipes of their blades. She thrust her axe gracefully upwards, shattering the jaw of one, then swung it around to split the skull of the second, bathing her in crimson.

As she went to wipe her eyes, the third slammed into her from behind. His arms, thick and corded with muscle, wrapped tightly around her, and squeezed with preterhuman strength. As she fought to break free, they rolled, tumbling off the edge of a steep embankment slick with mud. They slid with speed and force, pummeled by every branch and stone all the way down. But her adversary held firm. Suddenly the ground disappeared beneath them, and the girl briefly felt nothing but air before they plunged into the icy river below.

CHAPTER 25

The girl crawled out of the rushing water onto the sandy riverbank, coughed the water from her lungs, then collapsed onto her back, exhausted. She had finally escaped her adversary amid the raging current. Unfortunately, she had lost her weapon as well. She looked up into the purple and pink sky as the sun began to rise over the horizon, its first rays scattering through the trees. How long had it been since she had seen the light? Smelled the cool morning air? She breathed it in and closed her eyes. She felt drained, her strength depleted. Turned out she was still human after all.

She was awoken from her brief respite by the sudden sensation of gnarled hands around her throat. The man had returned. He crouched over her, squeezing her neck. She poked and clawed at his eyes and face, tearing away bits of flesh, but he was undeterred. He leaned into her face and opened his mouth wide, inhaling with a strained wheezing sound. The girl had the momentary sensation of being pulled from her body, then—

Bang!

A hole exploded from his head, raining down hot blood upon her. His grip released and he slumped over dead, pinning her beneath him. She heard the padding of feet upon sand, then felt the release of his weight as his body was lifted off her. She looked up to see a relieved expression on an unknown face as she passed into oblivion.

The girl awoke to the sensation of warmth and the smell of bacon. It reminded her of comfort, security…a home she couldn't remember. A face appeared in her mind—a man, kind and graying, and then another—a woman with round cheeks and a dimpled smile. They quickly vanished, and she couldn't recall the memory no matter how hard she tried. She felt pain and longing in their absence.

She opened her eyes. Sitting across from her was the man who had apparently saved her on the shore. He was removing a skillet of crackling bacon from the campfire that burned between them.

"Good morning! You slept for over twenty-four hours if you can believe it. I'll bet you're hungry."

The girl sat up in her sleeping bag, then quickly pulled it up to cover her tattered, threadbare clothing.

He averted his eyes. "All I had to…um, bury you in where the clothes the cult had cut off you. But there's a fresh set over there." He nodded towards the corner where a neatly folded shirt, jeans, hoodie, and shoes lay on a foot-stool. A muddy revolver lay on the ground next to it.

They were inside some type of structure, a slapdash construction of plywood, cardboard, and corrugated tin, loosely assembled on top of the foundational remains of what appeared to be an old log cabin. There was no door, just a wide opening and a large sheet of particle board rest-ing off to the side. The smoke from the fire rose up into the open sky through the few crisscrossing beams that passed for a ceiling.

"I don't know you," the girl said. Other faces had sparked recognition, but not his.

"No. I'm Noel. Noel Raddemer." He placed a few pieces of bacon on a plate and handed it to her. She hesitated only momentarily. She *was* starving.

"Whatever you want to know—if I know, I'll tell you. I'm not here to withhold information or dispense sage advice—even if I had any."

The girl was already on her third piece of bacon. It felt like she hadn't eaten in…how long?

"What happened to me? Where have I—"

"You were murdered," Noel said matter-of-factly.

It seemed impossible, but she somehow knew it to be true. Of course, she knew. She had fallen into darkness… had passed beyond the Veil. And somehow, had returned.

"How long?"

"It happened about three months ago."

Three months. She had been dead and gone from the world for three months. She swallowed, finishing off the last piece of bacon.

"And who are you? Why are you…helping me?"

"Like I said, I'm Noel. I used to work for the FBI. I headed up the counter cult division. We specialized in infiltrating and taking down dangerous cults. One of the stranger cases I investigated…well, let's just say it awoke something in me. Something I had long tried to forget. I became obsessed. Everything kept pointing back here. My bosses thought I had gone off the deep end. So, I quit. But I didn't stop investigating. Then one night, an envelope was slipped under my hotel door. It was a map to your body as well as instructions on what to do once I found you."

"And you didn't think that was strange?"

"After all I had seen over the past couple of years, no. In fact, it just confirmed that I had been on the right track all along. I wasn't..." He paused, appearing to push back against his emotions. "I wasn't crazy after all."

They both sat in silence for several moments. The only sound was the crackling of the fire.

"I don't remember who I am," the girl began. "Or know what I'm supposed to do now. I remember when I woke up, I had this, like...instinct. I didn't think about it, I just acted. I killed all those people. But they weren't even people, were they? Not really."

"This forest. It's cursed. Has been for a very long time. Something happened here. The monuments, the stone structures—they're all the result of an incursion into our world from another. And ever since, the intersection between worlds has become blurred. The Veil bleeds through."

The girl couldn't remember her own name, but she knew his words to be true. Even now, she could feel the tension between darkness and light within her very soul.

Noel tossed a few more sticks into the fire and continued. "True evil exists at the heart of these woods and throughout history men have sought it out. For some it's the promise of power. For others, the lure of forbidden knowledge. Then there are those who just revel in rebellion and blasphemy. William Darlington wasn't the victim that history paints him as. His daughter didn't just go missing. He was so desperate to learn the secrets of this place that he willingly offered her up."

The name stirred something within the girl's memory. She had heard this story, but not like this.

"But Darlington was a fool. Pacts with evil always come with a catch, and there's no escape clause. His whole family suffered for his sin. He brought the evil out of the woods into the town. And to this day, his legacy lives on.

"Through my investigation I learned of an underground cult thriving in secrecy in Darlington Hills. They call themselves the Disciples of the Veil. They are dedicated to continuing William Darlington's work and have devoted themselves in service to evil in these woods. Some members are more casual. They treat the whole thing like an exclusive social club. But others are much more devout. They open themselves up to the darkness, performing profane rituals, selling their very souls. It transforms them. Those are the ones you fought and killed."

Violet images flashed in the girl's mind. She recalled the sensation of axe on bone. "I know…I saw into them. Saw through the Veil. But how? Why am I a part of all this?"

"I told you I won't hold back the truth from you. But I want to be careful. You've been through a lot. If you're still struggling with your memory, I think it's best we ease into this."

"So, you're not even going to tell me my name?"

"You stand a better chance of regaining everything if it comes back naturally, through your own efforts. One you connect with one piece, the rest of them should begin to fall like dominoes. Right now, you should rest. Meditate."

The girl grew impatient. "I've been *resting* for three months. I feel anxious, like I should be doing something."

"Feel free to walk around a bit outside but stay inside the salt lines. I've done everything I can to consecrate this ground and keep it protected. Believe it or not, this humble abode rests on the remains of an old church. It seems at some point in the past, a few brave men pushed back against the evil, right here on this very spot. It didn't last, obviously, God rest their souls, but hopefully something of their righteous efforts remains."

He stood up, brushed off his jeans, and rolled up the sleeves of his red flannel shirt. "Well, I'll leave you to get dressed or whatever you need to do. If you need a bathroom, I've set up an enclosed space out back for you. There's a couple of buckets of clean water, towels, toilet paper. If there's anything else you need, just make a note of it and I'll see what I can do." He turned to go, then stopped. "By the way, you wouldn't happen to know what happened to my axe, would you?"

"Sorry. I lost it somewhere in the fight."

"Damn. Okay." He stepped outside and placed the panel of particle board over the doorway.

The sun shined bright in a gray sky, the air cool and brisk, when about an hour later, the girl stepped outside. She was fully dressed in her new clothes and about as clean as she could get with two buckets of cold water and a sponge. Noel had provided a small, handheld mirror for her, too, but even after staring several minutes at her reflection of steel blue eyes, round face, and short, choppy hair, she was no closer to remembering who she was or used to be.

"How'd those clothes work out for you?"

The girl turned around to see Noel emerging from the woods, carrying an armful of thick tree limbs. He dumped them into a large pile beside their makeshift shack. It looked even uglier and more unstable from the outside. Her eye was drawn to the weathered sign affixed above the opening. It read "Church of the Protectorate."

"Not bad. Thank you." In truth, the shirt was two sizes too big, the jeans were too short, and the soles were separating from the shoes, but she wasn't about to complain. Even though she still didn't know if she could trust this man, he had at least gone out of his way to make her comfortable. She pointed to the sign. "Original?"

"Yeah. It's great, isn't it? Found it just a few yards from here. Couldn't believe it was still in one piece. Just felt right to put it back up, you know?"

The girl walked out several yards until she came to the line of consecrated salt demarcating the edge of safety. It sparked a momentary recollection, but quickly faded.

Noel removed his gloves, wiped the sweat from his forehead, and approached her. "Take a few minutes. Enjoy the fresh air. But you should take the rest of the day to rest. We begin tonight."

"I'm sorry?"

"The Disciples will be making their next move. We have to stay ahead of them."

"Look, I want to be out there. I want to stop these monsters. But I'm going to need a little more from you. I need you to help me remember who I am."

"I told you. It's too risky. I need you focused. A total recall could leave you distracted, impaired. Too much is at stake."

"Is that what this is all about? Using me as some kind of weapon?"

"No. You don't understand—"

"I saw a girl out there. They took her. I knew her face. I need to know who she is to me. I need to know who I am, where I come from. My family. You want me to fight? Then help me remember what I'm fighting for."

Noel turned his back and began to walk away, then stopped and titled his head to the sky and sighed. "Okay," he said, looking back over his shoulder. "Let's see what you can remember...Becca Howl."

CHAPTER 26

The girl repeated it again. "My name is Becca Howl. My parents are Elyse and Matthew Howl. I have a sister named Whitley and a dog named Jake. I live at 1017 Windsor Drive. I love horseback riding and playing the piano."

"Anything?"

The girl slammed her fists into the dirt. "No! Nothing!" She stood up and paced back and forth. "It's all just... blank. I'm not connecting with any of it. Not a face, not a feeling, nothing. I don't get it. What if I'm damaged...like, permanently? What if I can't get any of it back?"

"I told you. It's going to take time. You can't force it."

She sat back down. "Let's try again," she insisted, closing her eyes.

"We've been at this for nearly three hours. Any more and you risk stripping it all of meaning, like when you repeat a word in your head too many times. I think the best strategy is to get a couple hours sleep. Rest up for tonight. Who knows? Maybe you'll wake up with an epiphany."

She didn't want to stop. It felt like quitting. But maybe he was right. Maybe she needed to turn her brain off for a bit, let it catch up.

Noel put another log on the fire and removed his boots. "It'll be okay. We'll get through this together."

The girl slipped into her sleeping bag and laid her head down. As she stared into the flames, her mind raced, trying to summon just a single memory from her previous life. Seconds later, she was fast asleep.

She awoke to the sound of singing. Beautiful, ethereal. She sat up and looked around. The fire had all but died, reduced to a faint orange glow. Noel still slept, snoring.

"Noel. Noel!" she whispered as loud as she could without being heard by whoever or whatever might be outside. He didn't budge. The singing seemed to get closer. The girl eased noiselessly out of her sleeping bag, slipped her hoodie over her head, and stepped outside. The air was still and surprisingly warm, and the night sky blue and clear and filled with stars. The singing continued. It sounded like a singular female voice. The girl kept walking, trying to home in on the source. The closer she got, she began to discern the words of the song—actually one word, repeated over and over again.

"...*Nara*..."

It awoke something in her. A notion. A feeling.

A realization.

She increased her pace until she came to the boundary and stopped. She looked into the impervious dark of the woods and called out, "Hello? Who's there?"

The girl's heart rate increased, and her breathing became quick and shallow.

"...*Nara*..."

It was a name...she knew that name...

The singing stopped. Then, out of the dark, someone appeared—a woman, pale and beautiful, wearing a gown of blue that seemed to glow in the moonlight. Her features were round and soft, and she appeared aged and ageless all at once. Her hair was white and braided and she wore a kind, dimpled smile.

"Don't be afraid," she said, extending her hand.

"Mom?" the girl asked, lip quivering.

"Nara. My dear, sweet, Nara. I've missed you so."

Nara. That was her name.

The walls of her memory came crashing down.

"Come on, sweetheart. Let me take you home."

Nara's eyes filled with tears. She looked down at the boundary of salt. She raised her foot.

"Nara, no! That's not your mother!" Noel shouted from somewhere behind her.

She looked back over her shoulder to see him racing towards her. "You lied to me!" she spat bitterly, then stepped over the boundary and took her mother's hand.

Noel screamed. "No!"

The mother embraced her daughter and flashed a wicked smile at Noel. "She's made her choice."

"Nara! Step back over the line, now!"

Nara watched in horror as her mother's beautiful visage began to melt away. Her form shifted and contorted with wet cracking sounds, completely shedding her matronly disguise to reveal a gnarled, corpse-like creature. Nara screamed as the being's clawed, gnarled hands wrapped around her, cutting into her flesh. She pushed against its grip, straining to break free as it began to drag her into the woods.

Noel reached down, grabbed a handful of salt, and tossed it into the eyes of the living corpse. It shrieked into the night with unholy furor as its face blistered and cracked. It released its hold on Nara and Noel leapt across the boundary, ramming into its midsection. The creature blindly flailed and slashed as they both crashed into the dirt. Nara watched as Noel reached into his shirt, removed a silvery, burnished cross, and plunged it into the creature's face. With a final, bloodcurdling shriek, it swelled into a bulbous, distended mass before exploding into a fetid glob of flesh and viscera.

Noel wiped a chunk from his face, then crawled back over the boundary line and vomited. He rose on his knees, trying to catch his breath. He stared back at the remains as they dissolved into the dirt. "I can't believe it. An actual necrocast. This is huge. It totally validates my theory that a coven of Neph—"

"You lied to me!"

Noel turned around to see Nara's face wet with tears. She looked him directly in the eyes. "Stay the hell away from me!"

"Nara, wait! I'm sorry! I...I wasn't trying to hurt you. I only wanted—"

She pointed her finger at his face. "I don't know you, I don't trust you, and I want nothing to do with you!" She spun around and stormed off into the night.

CHAPTER 27

Nara rounded the corner of Pike Street and stopped. She could see it now, just a couple blocks away. Her memory was slowly coming back, but it was still a bit of a mess, full of holes and missing pieces. But one thing she knew for certain—the way home.

After running out on Noel, she had wandered the forest for a little under an hour before coming out on the east side near the highway. She'd followed it up for two miles to the truck stop to make use of the bathroom and water fountain, doing her best to keep her face hidden beneath her hood. Flyers of her face and two other girls were pasted everywhere, right next to "wanted" posters of Noel. It was like she'd stepped out of one alternate universe into another.

From there it had been a short mile and a half walk to her neighborhood. But now, all of a sudden, her nervous excitement turned to fear. What if her dad wasn't happy to see her? What if he'd already mourned, moved on...glad to be unburdened of his freak daughter? She'd come all this way. Survived death and monsters. But these next few steps seemed the hardest.

"You're back."

Nara jumped and spun her head around, searching for the source of the voice. To her right, a porch light lit up. A small, hunched over form peaked out of the screen door.

Nara squinted. A name rose from her memory. "Mrs. Pulaski?"

"I warned you, didn't I?" she said, agitated.

"What?"

"I warned you. But you didn't listen. No one listens. It hasn't stopped, though. Damned thing still comes around, especially at night."

Dogs barked from within the house.

"Keeps my boys up." She turned her head back inside. "Hush now!"

At that moment, Nara noticed a white substance lining the outside of the woman's house. *Oh, my God.* She bent down and rubbed it between her fingers, then put it to her lips. *Salt.* It was coming back to her now. She had seen Mrs. Pulaski doing this the day she…she was with somebody? Who had she been with?

"Don't go messing with my circle, now!"

Nara stood. Her head swam. Was it all a big coincidence? "You don't happen to know a Noel Raddemer, do you?" she blurted out, only half joking.

"A who and a what?"

"Never mind," she said, bemused and perplexed. She took a deep breath and began her final steps towards home. She didn't even get five feet.

"Wait!" Mrs. Pulaski called out. "Did you say Raddemer?"

Nara stopped and turned around. "Yeah…"

Mrs. Pulaski stepped out of her doorway into the full glare of the porch light, tightening the belt of her yellow robe. "The Raddemers. Sad, sad story. Whole family just massacred. Except for that poor boy. The only survivor. What was his name? Nick? Neal? My husband used to teach him Sunday school."

Her stomach lurched. "N—Noel?"

"That was it. Noel. Good kid. But the boy was never the same after that."

Nara staggered backwards as the world began to spin.

"You okay out there?"

That was the last thing she heard before she hit the pavement.

Nara sipped on hot coffee as Mrs. Pulaski's two German shepherds, Max and Bull, stared at her, tails wagging.

"They like you," Mrs. Pulaski said, leaning back in her creaky recliner and muting the TV with her remote.

"I've never really been around dogs. Never owned one."

"That's too bad. Every little girl should have a puppy." She scratched Max, or possibly Bull, behind the ear. "So, you feeling better?"

"Yes, thank you. I don't know what happened to me. My head's been a little…" she said, making a twirling motion with her finger.

"Well, you've been through a lot. It's to be expected."

Nara leaned forward. "How do you know what I've been through?"

"You've been gone a while, right? Three months? Tells me you've been through something."

Nara leaned back again. How could one person be so irritating and yet so delightful all at once?

"I know you were headed home, but your father's not there. He's been staying over with his lady friend quite a bit. Can't say I like her."

Nara took the news like a punch to the gut. She hated the idea of him suffering, but some part of her had an image in her head of her father sitting by the living room window, waiting up every night for her to come home. But maybe her fears were true. Maybe her father *was* moving on. She stared into her coffee cup.

"You sure you don't want me to call the police? Or an ambulance?"

"I'm sure. I don't think…I don't think I'm ready for all that yet."

"Don't blame you. You just don't know who you can trust anymore. Right, boys?"

The dogs barked as if in agreement. And why not? Would hardly be the strangest thing Nara had experienced over the past two days.

"When you say you…*see* things—"

Mrs. Pulaski interrupted her. "Not things. Spirits and the like. Have ever since my husband passed, going on fourteen years now. I like to think it was his parting gift to me. Or curse, knowing him. He had always been the more spiritual one. Never shut up about it. He always said this town was different, that it stood on the edge of a door-way. He called it—"

"The Veil," Nara finished for her.

The old woman leaned back in her chair and re-peated, "The Veil."

The air felt suddenly close and heavy.

"You mentioned the Raddemers. What happened?"

"Your father never told you about it?"

"No. I've never heard of them."

"Strange. It was a pretty big deal. But the bad things that happen here do tend to disappear down the collective memory hole."

"What can you tell me?"

Mrs. Pulaski rose from her recliner. "Wait here."

She disappeared down the dark hallway and returned a few minutes later with an old newspaper. She dropped it in Nara's lap before returning to her chair. Dated August 2005, the headline read *"Family Killed in Brutal Slaying, Oldest Son, 16, Survives."*

"The mother, father, the two younger boys. It was like they had all been torn from the inside out," Mrs. Pulaski said, almost at a whisper.

Nara scanned the article, "And they never found out who did it? Or why?"

"Oh, they tried pinning it on a couple of unfortunate souls, but nothing stuck. The boy who lived—Noel—had been so traumatized that he wasn't of any help. There were so many strange things about the case that the police couldn't make heads or tails of it." She locked eyes with Nara. "Your father could tell you. He was there."

Nara wasn't sure what Mrs. Pulaski was trying to suggest, but she let it pass for now.

"What kind of strange things?"

"Read the article. There's a couple of details that made it in there before the official story got scrubbed of all inconvenient facts."

Nara scanned the rest of the article. "Wait. So, there was someone else there? A girl. She was murdered, too, but wasn't part of the family. It says here they have yet to identify her."

"And they never have. No records, no family, nothing except what she left behind. Just flesh and blood."

Suddenly the dogs' ears perked up. They barked and stood to attention. Mrs. Pulaski leapt from her chair and peered out the curtains. "Son of a bitch."

"What is it?" Nara jumped up and joined the woman at the window. Outside, encircling the boundary, stood several figures in black hooded robes.

Nara gasped. "Oh, my God."

"Listen. You need to go out the back. Crossover through the neighbor's yard and just start running and don't look back until you get to your father."

"I don't know where Amanda lives!"

"Just get to the Sheriff's station. I'm about to put in a call. Believe me, they'll get his ass out of bed."

"What about you?"

"Don't worry about me. If the boundary doesn't hold them off, I've got my boys to look out for me. And if they're not up to the challenge—" she whipped out a shotgun from behind the curtain and pumped it, loading the chamber, "—then Big Sister's got my back. Now, go!"

"Mrs. Pulaski...thank you."

Nara burst out the back door and hit the ground running. She crossed the backyard in just a few strides and quickly scaled the fence separating Mrs. Pulaski's yard with her neighbor's. She felt her adrenaline pumping, her senses coming alive. It was the same sensation she'd felt when she'd battled the cult. She sped past the neighbor's house and came out on the next street over.

A shotgun blast rang out behind her. Nara closed her eyes, quickly praying for Mrs. Pulaski's safety, but kept running and didn't stop.

CHAPTER 28

Nara hid in the shadows behind the hair salon across from the police station, trying to catch her breath. As far as she knew, she hadn't been followed. But then, she didn't know how they had tracked her to Mrs. Pulaski's in the first place. She had to assume they could be anywhere, even among the police, so going to them without her father present was not an option. Sirens blared in the distance, but she hadn't seen his cruiser arrive or depart, so she remained hidden for now and waited—assuming the old woman was true to her word.

Minutes felt like hours. Her body remained tense and alert—ready to fight or flee at a moment's notice—right up until the moment she saw him. He had finally arrived at the station and was stepping out from his vehicle. Memories of walks in the park, stories at bedtime, and birthday dinners all came flooding back at the sight of his face. But the moment was bittersweet. His eyes were tired, his face heavy with concern. It looked like he had aged ten years since she saw him last.

Her heart began to race, and her hands trembled in anticipation. She wanted nothing more at that moment than to hug him and tell him that she was okay, that he wouldn't have to worry any more. She stepped from the shadows, pulled down her hood, and opened her mouth to shout—

—and felt a hand clamp over her face and another around her arm, dragging her back behind the salon. She wrangled free and twisted around, fists raised, ready to pummel her assailant with her bare hands.

"Whoa, whoa, whoa! It's just me!" Noel said, hands raised in mock surrender.

Nara reared back, clenching her fist. "You're not helping your case."

"I know, I know. Just, please. Hear me out."

"You're preventing me from seeing my father again. You've got ten seconds."

"That's the thing. You can't go back to him. Not yet."

She peeked around the corner towards the police station to see that he'd already gone inside. "And why is that? Wouldn't be because your face is plastered all over town, and you know I can lead him right to you, would it?"

Noel hung his head. "Look, you have every right to be mad at me. If you really want to go over there and turn me in, I won't stop you. But you'd be making a huge mistake."

"And why is that?"

"For one, the Disciples are everywhere. More than likely, they've got a man or two inside the department."

"Already considered that. Is that all you got?"

"You'd be putting her at risk." Noel motioned to something over Nara's shoulder. She turned around to see a neon pink flyer affixed to a telephone pole, printed with the word "Missing" in big bold letters. And below that, a photograph. A face. The girl she had seen being dragged into the woods. The girl who meant more to her than any living person beside her dad.

"You wouldn't be standing here right now if it weren't for her. She put it all on the line for you."

The final barriers to Nara's memories collapsed. Hazy was it—the missing piece that connected all other pieces. The span of their entire friendship replayed in the theater of her mind, all the smiles and the tears, good times and bad. Sneaking into punk shows. The time Dad pretended to arrest them for skipping school. Prank calling her brother Simon to trick him into thinking Laura Sittler had a crush on him.

Simon.

She remembered his face as he comforted her on the steps of Darlington High…and again as he lunged forward to thrust a knife into her belly. She shuddered, then stumbled to her knees in a cold sweat.

Noel moved swiftly to catch her. "Whoa! You okay?"

"I remember…I remember everything…Hazy. We've got to find her."

"I know," he said, helping her to her feet. "We will."

Nara looked back to the police station wistfully. Her reunion would have to wait.

"Something's not right," Nara said as they approached Elijah's second floor apartment. It was nearly 2 a.m. and the front door was wide open.

Noel stopped in his tracks. "We're too late. Let's go. Time for plan B."

"No! Elijah's my…friend. I have to see if he's okay."

"This is not a good idea. It could be a trap. They could be watching us right now."

"Then stay here and be my lookout. Just let me handle this, okay?"

Nara sprinted up the stairs and paused at the doorway. It was pitch black inside. "Elijah?"

No response.

She glanced back down at Noel who looked around nervously while trying to remain inconspicuous. She turned back towards the doorway and called out again.

"Elijah?"

She stepped inside. The living room was completely dark, but by the outside light she could see it was in complete disarray. A light flickered from the next room. She heard something…a sound like sobbing. "Elijah?"

A voice, faint and ragged, called back. "Who's there?"

Nara sped around the corner. Elijah sat in the middle of the kitchen floor, hair matted with blood, cradling his unconscious father. Chairs lay overturned amid shattered plates. The overhead light hung loose, barely holding on.

"Oh, my God! What happened?"

Elijah's squinted in the strobing light. "Nara?"

"What can I do?"

"I think he had a heart attack. He tried to fight them off. I called 911."

Nara cleared away some debris and went down on one knee beside them, checking his father's pulse. "He's still hanging on. Are you okay?" She reached to check his head wound. It didn't seem serious, but he was clearly in shock.

"Nara…how are you here? I thought you were dead. I dreamed about you…all the time."

"Elijah, I need to know what happened."

"I tried. I tried to be strong. They were angry. I didn't care what they did to me. But they threatened to kill her. They…" he broke down, weeping. "They showed me video. She was screaming. I…I'm sorry. I had to…I had to give it to them."

Sirens blared in the distance.

"It's okay. Help's on the way. Just stay with your dad."

"What about Hazy? This is all my fault."

"No. It's not. I'm going to get her back. That's a promise." She stood and turned to go.

"I'm sorry," he said, wiping his eyes. "For what I did to you. All of it. I'm a terrible person."

Noel suddenly appeared in the doorway. "We've got to go. Now!"

"You've got a good heart, Elijah." She followed Noel out of the apartment. "You were right. It was here," she said as they bounded down the stairs.

They fled back over the fence just as police and paramedics converged on the scene.

CHAPTER 29

The wet sheen covering Ridley Street was suffused with color cast from the neon "Open All Night" sign in the window of Pitch Black Books.

"For when you absolutely have to summon a demon at three in the morning," Noel said, popping up the collar of his jacket and tugging down on the brim of the baseball cap he'd pilfered from the garbage. "You ready for this?"

"I don't like this place. Have never liked it. The way it makes me feel."

"A lot of dark energy here. It's like an antennae for evil. You think you can handle it?"

"Right now, all I care about is getting Hazy back. Nothing else matters."

"Okay, then. Let's do this."

They stepped in from the icy drizzle and were greeted to the sound of chiming crystals. A curly, red-haired teen, engrossed in a mobile app game, barely glanced up from his phone to acknowledge them. He offered a half-hearted, mumble-mouthed, "Welcometopitchblack."

Nara pretended to peruse the periodicals while Noel approached the counter, trying to keep his head low. "Uh, hi. It's Derek, right? Me and my associate just drove in from out of town. We were hoping to uh…peruse the VIP room, if you know what I mean."

Derek remained transfixed to his phone and delivered a monotone, memorized response. "Access to the Vault is only during daytime hours and by appointment only."

Noel leaned in, resting his elbow on the counter. "That's the thing. We made this appointment last week. Tessa made special arrangement for us because of my busy schedule. She directed us to just let you know when we got in, and that you would ring her up to meet us here."

Derek finally looked up. "That doesn't sound right. Wait, do I know you?"

Noel put on a front of exasperation. "Are you telling me we drove all the way from Tallahassee, only for you to tell me that you forgot about our appointment?"

"I didn't forget. I'm just saying—"

"Oh, you didn't forget. You're just being difficult? Tessa will be very interested to hear about this."

"Sir, I really don't know what you're talking about."

Noel slammed his hand on the counter. "Then I suggest you call Tessa right now and get this sorted out. I happen to be prepared to drop a very substantial sum tonight, and I think she would be very upset if she were to miss out on our business."

Derek appeared to weigh his odds before finally relenting. "I'll be right back." He stepped out from behind the counter and disappeared somewhere among the maze of shelves.

"What do you think?" Nara whispered at his side.

"I think I got to him. He's definitely calling her. The question is, does she answer, and if she does, is she curious enough to come down here herself, or does she just call the police to have us removed?"

"And if she comes down here?"

Noel opened his jacket ever so slightly to reveal a revolver tucked into his inner pocket. It appeared to be the same one she had seen lying in his shelter. "We improvise."

"Are you're positive she's part of the cult?"

"One hundred percent. We just have to hope she's far enough up the chain to have details on Hazy."

"Sir?"

They both turned around. Derek had returned.

"She said she'll be down as soon as possible. Could be up to half an hour or so. You're free to enjoy come complimentary coffee in our lounge area while you wait."

"Great, Derek. Thank you. Now…" Noel said, removing the revolver from his jacket, aiming it at the teen. "… give me your phone."

Derek froze, his face barely registering an expression.

Nara grabbed Noel by the arm, whispering through clenched teeth and a fake smile. "Noel? What are you doing?"

"Just drop the phone on the ground, okay? That's it, good kid. Now slowly turn around and interlock your fingers behind your head."

"Aunt Tessa's going to be so pissed. You may as well shoot me."

Noel picked up the phone and shove it in his pocket. "Don't tempt me, Derek. Now, hands behind your head. Move!"

Noel shoved the point of the barrel in his back and directed him to the men's room "Get in. You try to get out before I say it's okay, you even make a sound, I will come back here and shoot you in the kneecaps. Got it?" Noel shoved him in and slammed the door.

"That's overkill, don't you think?" Nara said, crossing her arms. "I don't think Ron Weasley here is a threat to anyone but himself."

"The key to maintaining control of any situation is to keep the variables to a minimum. He's a variable. I need him contained." Noel scanned the area. He reached for the nearest bookcase and wiped an entire row of books onto the floor before ripping the shelf from its brackets. He returned to the restroom door and shoved the shelf up underneath the handle.

"There. That should hold him for now."

Nara sighed in exasperation. "So, now what?"

"We wait. Coffee?

"May as well have a seat," Noel said as Nara paced back and forth. "Rest while you can." He took a sip of his coffee and leaned back in the lounge's plush antique couch.

"I can't relax here. It's all…getting in my head." she said, eyes wandering up and down the spines of hundreds of pagan texts, spell books, and spirit guides. The concentration of so much darkness in one place unsettled her. She could feel it hewing at the corners of her mind, probing for weakness.

"I spent so much of my life at war with myself, on guard against the evil I felt in my own heart. Yet this place is filled with people who dedicated their lives to searching it out."

Noel's face grew dark. "'The LORD saw how great the wickedness of the human race had become on the earth, and that every inclination of the thoughts of the human heart was only evil all the time.' Genesis 6:5. That was right before the great flood. I'd say the Earth is overdue for another cleansing," he stated grimly.

Nara finally ceased her pacing and sat down in the green velvet chair across from Noel, restlessly rubbing her hands over her knees.

Noel leaned forward. "I know you're not comfortable. As soon as this woman tells us what we need to know, we're out of here."

Nara bit down on her bottom lip. "There's something else."

Noel sat his coffee down. "Okay."

"I, uh. I heard about your family. About what happened when you were younger."

"Oh," he said, taken aback. "So that's how you spent your couple of hours away from me? Digging up my past. Seeing if I'm who I say I am?"

"No. It wasn't like that at all. Is it true, though?"

Noel rubbed his bristled chin. "Yeah. It's true." His voice sounded far away.

"I'd like to hear it from you if you don't mind. Who was the girl?"

Noel pursed his lips. "Oh, boy. Sounds like you got the full download."

"Mrs. Pulaski."

"Ah. Makes sense. I knew her husband. He was a very devout man, but not your cut and paste church deacon. The guy had a very hands-on approach to spiritual matters."

"Like salt rings?"

Noel smirked. "Exactly."

"Why didn't you tell me you were from Darlington Hills?"

"Would it have made a difference?"

"I don't know. But you promised me you wouldn't hold back, that you'd tell me whatever I wanted to know. So, I want to know. Help me understand."

Noel breathed deep. "I was sixteen years old. I was on a family hike with my parents and two little brothers, Nick and Neal. My parents loved the outdoors. Real back-to-nature types. Seemed like we were out there in the woods every weekend. Well, this particular Saturday, we'd just set up the tent. Dad was getting the fire going, getting ready to fry the fish we'd caught that day.

"All of a sudden, we hear crying. We're alone out there, not another soul for miles, and it's pitch black all around us. We get a little freaked out. But my dad puts on a brave face, grabs his flashlight, and goes looking. Me and my brothers follow right behind. We don't get very far. Maybe twenty, thirty yards from camp, and there she is. This girl. She's just sitting there, huddled against a tree. She's young, around my age. And she's terrified. The other weird thing was…she was wearing this blue, old timey dress. She just seemed so out of place. But I remember thinking how pretty she was. She just looked at me with these big, blue, sad eyes." Noel paused, appearing to push back against a sudden swell of emotions.

"And then…then we notice she's bleeding. She was pregnant and the baby was on its way. So, Dad picks her up and carries her back to camp. Mom's freaking out, trying to get a call out on her cell phone, but it was basically useless. You can barely get a call out of that forest now, never mind back then. So, it becomes clear pretty quick that my parents are going to have to deliver the baby. This whole time, this girl never says a word. I felt so sorry for her. I didn't know what else to do, so I just sat and held her hand while she gave birth. She kept her eyes on me the all the way through.

"Then, almost as soon as the baby is out, we hear this loud, ungodly shriek."

A lump formed in Nara's throat as she sensed the story careening towards its terrible, inevitable end.

"While everyone was trying to figure out what they had just heard, the girl squeezes my hand and pulls me close and whispers in my ear. We heard the shriek again. And I remember looking up and seeing this...thing crawl out of the forest. In my head, I thought, 'That's the devil.' So, I grabbed the baby, and I ran. I ran and I ran through the dark all the way to the ranger's station and never looked back. Then the police came. And they took the baby and I never saw it again. Sometime the next day, an officer came and told me that they had found the remains of my family. The girl too. And that officer just sat and held onto me as I cried. I must have gone on for hours. I'll always be grateful to him for that."

For the first time since beginning his story, Noel looked up and made eye contact with Nara, communicating words unspoken. Realization kindled in her mind, igniting a blaze of emotion. Her eyes brimmed with tears.

"What did the girl whisper to you?" she asked, voice trembling.

"She told me your name and made me promise to watch over you."

Nara doubled over and began to weep. Her entire life she had longed for the truth, hoping it would give her closure and heal whatever was damaged inside her. Instead, it just broke her heart.

Noel place a single hand on her shoulder.

"This was not how I imagined telling you…under these circumstances, in a place like this. But here we are."

Nara rose up and wiped her eyes. "Who was she?"

"I've spent a long time trying to figure that out. She just seemed to come from nowhere." His jaw clenched. "This won't be easy to hear." He paused. "Or believe."

"I can take it."

Noel opened his mouth to speak but was interrupted by the chimes of someone coming through the front door.

"Derek?" a woman's voice called out.

Noel rose from his seat and mouthed to Nara, "You ready?

She wiped her eyes again and nodded.

"Derek?" Tessa called again as she rounded the corner. She took one look at Noel and turned to run.

Noel cocked the gun and pointed. "I wouldn't."

Tessa halted and spun around, her face red. "What the hell is this?!"

Noel grimaced. "I think you know."

Noel motioned to Nara. She took his cue and ripped Tessa's keys from her hand, then proceeded to lock the front door, turn down the lights, and shut off the "Open All Night" sign.

"Where's Hazy?"

"Hazy? I don't know what you're talking about," she said, stone faced.

"Don't play games with me. She was in here just a couple days ago. I know you're with the Disciples."

Tessa glanced over Noel's shoulder at the sound of faint creaking emanating from the rear exit.

Noel tensed. "What was that?"

Tessa smirked. "I didn't hear anything."

He leaned his head towards Nara, keeping his eyes locked on Tessa. "Watch her. I'm going to check it out." He lowered the gun and backed away through the lounge before disappearing around the corner.

Nara held her focus on Tessa. She looked harmless enough, but if she was connected to the Disciples, there was no telling what she was capable of.

"You don't belong with him, you know. He's poison," Tessa asserted.

"Shut up."

"We've waited so long to find you. You belong with us. With your family."

"My family? Are you sick? You had me murdered."

Tessa gloated. "You have it wrong, Nara Shadespawn."

The utterance of that name chilled Nara's spine. "Don't call me that!"

More noise—creaking and clanging—sounded from the rear of the store.

"Noel?" Nara called out, keeping her eyes on Tessa. "Are you okay? Please hurry!"

Tessa continued. "The ritual that night was to be the fulfillment of an oath made nearly two hundred years ago. You are the bridge between the two worlds—a conjunction of flesh and spirit. The bloodletting was essential to part the Veil. When you fled, the process was interrupted. Mistakes were made. Your death was an error—a misguided act of impulse. The offender has since been disciplined. Isn't that right, Simon?"

Nara turned to see Noel shuffling forward, hands up, nose and lips bloodied. Simon followed, glasses askew, knife in one hand, revolver in the other.

Noel spat blood. "Discount Ted Bundy got the drop on me."

Simon slugged Noel on the back of the head with the butt of the revolver. Noel fell hard to his knees. Nara rushed to his side, placing her hand over the fresh bleeding wound.

Simon joined Tessa. She reached out her hands and affectionately wrapped them around his cheeks. "I'm so proud of you, Simon. Your efforts to redeem yourself have not gone unnoticed. This is your chance to prove your true worth to the family and put an end to Raddemer. Spill his blood and your reconsecration into the Disciples will be one step closer."

Simon reached into his pocket and removed a single bullet. He loaded the chamber and pointed it at Noel. Noel glared back.

"You can't do this, Simon! Look at me!" Nara pleaded. "I know you. Whatever mistakes you've made, this isn't you. It's never too late to turn back. If not for me, then do it for Hazy."

Simon scowled, sweat beading on his forehead. He cocked the hammer.

"Praise the Void!" Tessa said, closing her eyes and lifting her hands in obscene reverence.

The gun fired.

Blood sprayed as Tessa's body fell.

The revolver clattered to the floor.

CHAPTER 30

Nara finished cleaning Noel's head wound and applying bandages from the store's emergency first aid kit. "Best I can do until you see a doctor."

"Thanks. Now I gotta deal with this."

She watched him tuck the reclaimed revolver into his belt and walk over to Simon, who was in the process of draping his jacket over Tessa's body.

"Well done. You just snuffed out our only chance of finding Hazy. I'm guessing if they'd let you back into the inner circle, you wouldn't be here."

"You're welcome for saving your life," Simon retorted.

"You didn't save it. You just decided not to take it. Big difference."

Simon hung his head.

"Look, I appreciate the change of heart, but I still don't trust you." Noel extended his hand. "Whatever rounds you have left, I want them."

Simon glowered. He reached into his pocket and emptied his hand into Noel's.

"Three bullets. That's it?"

"That's it."

Noel loaded them into the chamber and placed the revolver inside his jacket.

"Noel," Nara said. "Can you give us a minute?"

"Sure, but make it quick. Now we've got to come up with Plan C. I'll dig through the office to see if I can find anything that'll give us something to go on."

As he walked away, he pointed a finger towards Simon. "Keep your distance." He disappeared down the hallway, leaving them alone.

Simon slouched, staring down into the puddle of blood at his feet.

Moments passed before Nara broke the silence.

"I just want to know why."

"You wouldn't understand."

"What did Tessa mean about you making a mistake?"

"It doesn't matter."

"That's not for you to decide. The least you could do after what you did is give me some kind of an explanation."

"I'd rather you just put a bullet in my head and be done with it."

"There's been enough killing. I deserve to know, Simon."

He finally looked up, righteous defiance in his eyes. "I did it to save you, okay? It sounds totally insane, but it's true! If they had caught you and taken you back to the circle and completed the ritual, you wouldn't be you anymore. I...I did what I did to save you from something worse than death."

"Do you have any idea how that sounds?"

"Of course, I do! But don't you get it? The answer was right there in your journal. When you showed it to me, I couldn't believe it. You had basically laid out the conditions for your resurrection without even realizing it. The correct phase the moon, the position of the stars and planets, it was all there. Afterwards...I took the journal, hid it from Dargo. When you didn't come back right away, I pored over it, trying to find some clue that I may have missed. I tried everything...I..."

For a brief moment, she caught a glimpse of that same sensitive boy who comforted her on the steps of Darlington High, who took her for coffee, and made her laugh. The sad truth was, she didn't hate him as much as she wanted to. She wanted to tell him she forgave him, that she was alive right now and that's all that mattered.

But it wasn't all that mattered. Some things were never okay, no matter the intention, no matter the outcome.

"And what about the other girls? Becca and Melani. Did you kill them too?"

"No, they were a mistake. The Disciples had been searching for you for a long time. But they had to wait until you turned seventeen to perform the ritual. The number is significant to them. They had narrowed the list of candidates to four girls your age who'd been adopted. Becca and Melani just happened to be the first ones on the list. You were the last. When neither survived the ceremony, they were ready to move on to the next girl. But when Dargo saw what happened to you in the woods, he knew it was you."

Nara grew furious. "And so, you manipulated me... took advantage of my trust! You took me out there and abandoned me to them, knowing what was going to happen!"

"You're right. There's no forgiving what I did."

"Then why did you do it?"

Simon hesitated, looking down at the floor again. "For family."

Nara blinked. "What does that even mean?"

"I was in too deep. I was trying to protect them. But the moment I did what I did, I damned them all." He slumped to his knees. "I can't save her, Nara. Tonight, they're going to finish what William Darlington started. They will offer one of their own to the evil in the woods. They've chosen Hazy. That will be my punishment for taking you from them. I turned their messiah into their angel of death."

"Wait. You said 'one of their own.' What did you mean by that?"

"Simon learned the truth," Noel's voice cut in. "Didn't you, Simon? That's how Dargo recruited you. He told you that he was your real father. And Hazy's. And when you confronted your mother over it, she left in shame."

"Simon? Is that true?"

His silence was the only confirmation she needed.

"But that's not all," Noel continued. "There are stories that following his family's demise, William Darlington fathered more children with women of ill-repute. Dargo believes himself to be a direct descendant of Darlington, and by extension, Simon and Hazy as well. Just as William Darlington offered his daughter to evil, so will Dargo."

"But Darlington's daughter ultimately escaped," Simon muttered, his expression morose. "They won't let that happen again."

"Wait. What do you mean escaped? I thought his daughter was lost or sacrificed or something."

"The history lesson can wait," Noel blurted, glaring at Simon. "Right now, we need a plan."

Simon eyes lit ups. He jumped to his feet. "That's it."

"That's what?" Nara asked.

"I know how we're going to find Hazy." He approached Noel with purpose in his step and looked him in the eye. "But first, you have to tell her. If you don't I will." He turned his eyes towards Nara. "She's not our pawn. She deserves to know," he said, contritely reiterating her own words.

Nara directed her attention towards Noel. "Does this have to do with what you were going to tell me earlier… before we were interrupted?"

Noel's hand cupped his chin as if deep in thought. "It took a long time to unravel this, to finally understand and accept the truth of what happened. Before we found her out there in the woods that night, your mother—your birth mother—had been so desperate to escape her fate that, either through sheer will or a weakening in the barrier, she physically pierced the Veil and slipped through. But she didn't just cross over distance. It seems that in the Veil, time has no meaning. When she emerged, only moments had passed for her, but nearly two centuries had passed for the world. She had finally escaped the evil she had been bound to, but only long enough to deliver you. She had done the impossible…risked it all to give her daughter a fighting chance." Noel paused, placing his hand on Nara's shoulder. "Nara…your mother was Sara Darlington, the lost daughter of William Darlington."

CHAPTER 31

Hazy laughed. Maybe it was the drugs. Maybe it was the fact that she had no idea where she was or where she was going. The past few...hours? days? weeks?...had been nothing but a confusing, disjointed haze. She had become completely unmoored from reality. She'd imagined her brother wielding a gun, had encountered men with glowing eyes, and had even hallucinated Nara, back from the dead, killing monsters with an axe. If she didn't laugh, she'd probably lose her mind. If she hadn't already.

All was dark as she felt herself pushed, shoved, and dragged to who knows where. They'd covered her head with a sack or something...whoever they were. At some point before that, they'd stripped her out of her clothes and dressed her in a flimsy, short red gown that left little to the imagination. Out here in the freezing cold, she mused, someone was getting a good show.

Whatever was going to happen tonight, she at least had enough of her mental faculties to realize that she was probably going to die. It may have been the constant injection of drugs talking, but she thought she was actually okay with it. Nothing good had come from her life. Her mother had split. Her dad was most likely dying, and her brother had joined a cult. Throw in a dead best friend, and her brief existence had been one miserable disappointment after another.

They came to stop—finally. She imagined her feet had been worn down to bloody stumps. They hadn't even had the common decency to put a pair of shoes on her before they'd dragged her over every rock, tree limb, and pine needle in Darlington Hills. *Assholes.*

They pulled the bag from her head, and after her eyes regained their focus, she beheld a twisted, nightmarish version of her class field trip to Veilwood Forest. As before, Mr. Dargo stood perched atop the remnants of some ancient stone structure, a book open in his hands. Only this time he was dressed in crimson robes, and he wasn't holding a history text. There was no mistaking the bright red cover of Nara's journal. *Damn you, Elijah. You had one job.*

Instead of an audience of students, black robed cultists stood in a wide circle bearing torches. Hands pushed Hazy forward, directing her towards an elevated stone platform next to Dargo. Jutting up from it was a thick, wooden beam. Her arms were pulled back and bound to it. There was nothing she could do to stop them. She had lost all will to resist. She simply rolled her head towards Dargo and laughed.

He stared back with soulless eyes and said, "Bless you, my daughter, for the sacrifice you are about to make."

I've lost my freakin' mind. My history teacher just called me his daughter.

Dargo turned to face his unholy congregation. "And now, we shall perform the ceremonial bloodletting required to initiate our dark communion."

From somewhere beyond the edges of Hazy's blurred vision, two figures emerged—one in black, the other, it seemed, was wearing nothing at all. Through the girl's red swollen eyes and make-up smeared cheeks, Hazy recognized her face. Britney Kohl. And the one leading her up to the platform—Violet.

Britney sobbed, pleading for her life.

"Why is this one offered this infernal night?" Dargo formally inquired.

"Apostasy. She has betrayed us." Violet declared, her voice seething with contempt.

"Thank you, faithful daughter."

What? How many damn kids does this guy think he has?

He then handed her a curved, gleaming dagger. "This honor belongs to you."

Britney wailed. "Please, no! I'll do anything! Please!"

Violet slid the dagger across the Britney's throat in one swift, clean motion. A stream of crimson cascaded down her bare chest. She sputtered and choked, showering Hazy in a spray of blood.

Britney's lifeless body collapsed at Hazy's feet.

Like the shock of a frigid douse of ice water, Hazy was shaken from her stupor. She struggled against her bonds, but her efforts were futile.

All fell silent. Before her was nothing but impenetrable darkness. Dargo looked to the journal and began to chant.

CHAPTER 32

The basement beneath Pitch Black, dubbed the Vault, was basically a glorified concrete box. Nara, Simon, and Noel had reached the bottom of the creaky, wooden stairs to a musty odor and a series of shelving units, two rows deep, lining the walls on all sides. The shelves brimmed with boxes of various shapes and sizes, interspersed with unknown artifacts and curiosities sealed in plastic bags. The center of the room was empty, save for a summoning circle painted onto the floor.

It had a negative effect on Nara almost instantly. She winced at the sudden onrush of dull, throbbing pain in her head.

"This was used for impromptu ceremonies, or for high paying customers who wanted to experience something a little more…authentic," Simon explained.

Nara clutched her stomach. "I think I'm going to be sick."

"That's why this has a good chance of working."

Nara was still having trouble accepting the idea that her mother had crossed time and space by passing through the shadowy realm of demons, but she needed it to be true if they were going to have any chance of saving Hazy.

"How do we know it's not already too late?"

"They just got their hands on your journal, which they needed to correctly perform the invocation. Dargo's big on dramatics too. Factor in their trip to the ruins, I'd say we've got about a half hour, maybe less before I start to get worried."

"Then hurry and get to it. I'm going shopping," Noel said and began striding up and down the rows of shelves, rummaging through boxes of relics.

Simon walked the perimeter of the circle. "First thing we need to do is negate some of these hexes." He removed a knife from his back pocket and sliced his palm. Blood welled to the surface.

Nara cringed.

"I'm a little short on art supplies at the moment," he stated. "And blood happens to grease the ethereal wheels." He knelt down and begin to paint over the enchantments along the edges of the circle. "Hopefully, this is where my obsession with this shit finally pays off."

"How long?"

"Just a few minutes. Then it's all up to you."

Everything depended on her ability to do something she didn't know how to do in order to pull off something she couldn't understand. *Great.*

She joined Noel at the far corner of the room, where he continued to pilfer the Pitch Black archives. He had strapped himself to the nines with knives, some kind of medieval-looking gauntlet, and a crossbow.

"What are you doing? You look ridiculous!"

"Do you want to materialize in the middle of a murderous cult empty handed?"

"I honestly hadn't thought that far ahead. I'm just hoping I don't vaporize us all just trying to get there."

"Have a look around. There's plenty of things to maim or kill with down here. Ancient ceremonial daggers, swords, a spear. Just find something that feels comfortable. You don't want anything too heavy or unwieldy in a close quarters fight."

"You sound like you're preparing for war."

"Nara, when your mother passed through the Veil, something followed her—the thing I saw that night. I believe it's been living in Darlington Hills ever since, hiding in human form, biding its time." Noel looked over her shoulder at Simon, still busy marking the circle. "I think it's one of them. I believe one of the Disciples is the monster who killed your mother…and my family. Just stay alert."

"I will," she said.

She turned to explore aisles, scoping the shelves for anything interesting. What did she know about weapons, though? All she knew was that—

She stopped. Something caught her attention on the middle rack closest to the wall. It seemed to almost…*call* to her. She approached it as it lay there out in the open, not contained within a box or wrapped in plastic. Only a simple tag hung from its handle. *Item #253.*

It was an axe. And not just any axe. Symbols like the ones from her journal were carved into its handle.

"What'd you find?" Noel asked from over her shoulder.

She turned to face him, the weapon resting in her hands. "It looks older, a little rougher, and it's got symbols etched in the handle, but I swear—"

His face fell. "Let me see that."

He took it from her hands, inspecting it.

He flipped it over, showing her the bottom of the handle. The initials N.R. were smooth and worn, but visible.

"N.R. for Niles Raddemer. It was my father's axe. I've kept it ever since. I had it until the night you came back..."

"I lost it in the fight. How is this possible? What does it mean?"

"I think it means this is going to work," Simon cut in, appearing behind them. He took the axe from Noel and ran his fingers across the etching. "These symbols...I recognize them. *Malleus Praecantrix*. It means 'Witch Hammer.' It's the name of an ancient weapon used to...well, kill witches."

Nara contorted her face. "Now I'm really confused."

"I think what he's trying to say is, this weapon has passed in and out of time," Noel added. "The etchings weren't here before, so clearly this version is from some point in the future."

Simon interjected. "But eventually, it ended up in the past, and was found and stashed away here."

Nara felt her brain turning to mush. "But the one I lost—?"

"Is still out there somewhere, waiting to be found," Simon explained.

"Wait! You hear that?" Noel raised his hand, signaling for them to be quiet. "Sirens."

"What? How did—?" Simon muttered.

"Wait here!"

Noel dashed back up the stairs and returned seconds later. "It was Derek! He got out!" He pointed a finger at Nara. "I told you we couldn't trust that punk!"

Simon leapt into position inside the circle. "We're out of time! Everybody in! Nara, you're up!"

"I'm not sure what I'm supposed to do!"

"Just close your eyes. Open yourself up to everything you've been trying to keep out. Trust yourself to be strong enough to resist the darkness. You can do this, Nara," Simon affirmed. "It's in your blood."

She closed her eyes and tried to concentrate. The blare of the sirens grew closer.

"I...I can't!"

"Hold up!" Noel reached into his pocket and placed something in Nara's hand—the silver pentacle necklace Hazy had given to her on her birthday.

"Use this. Focus on Hazy. Your friendship...what she means to you. Reach out through the noise and find her."

She nodded and took the necklace, holding it tight to her chest. She shut her eyes again and peered into the dark. And this time, welcomed it. Her pulse quickened. Her blood ran cold. Almost instantly they were there. Formless faces and dissonant whispers. They called to her, as they always did. She let go, surrendering to the seducing lure of the Veil, and reached out to Hazy. The world seemed to bend and shift around her, passing from light to shadow.

"You're doing it, Nara!" Simon exclaimed over the sudden rush and crackling of the air.

Forceful banging boomed from above, breaking Nara's concentration. *The police! They're here!*

"Stay focused. We're almost through!" Noel shouted.

She sensed the ground beneath her feet give way. She seized the powers of air and darkness for herself and bent them to her will.

The basement door burst open.

The Veil parted.

Her father's face was the last thing Nara saw as she departed the world of matter and light.

CHAPTER 33

Hazy closed her eyes and tried to focus on anything other than where she was and what was happening to her at that moment. She recalled simpler times from the past—fond memories of time spent with her dad, sneaking out at night with her brother, laughing and crying with Nara. But then, she would feel the wet, sticky sensation around her toes and be thrown back to reality. They had removed Britney's body, but her blood remained, pooled around Hazy's feet.

Dargo, still perched upon his stone pedestal to her left, had just completed another round of incomprehensible chanting. Violet remained at his side, basking in his evil glow. His words made her sick, their sharp, profane utterances like pinpricks in her brain. Whatever was happening, she wanted it to be over. If they were going to kill her, why not just do it already?

Dargo turned to his followers and extended his arms. "Almost two hundred years ago, our illustrious forebearer, William Darlington, sought out the secrets of these woods. As evidenced by the ruins beneath our feet, an ancient power, born out of the rebellion against the Heavens, once thrived here…that is, until the Day of Reckoning. But a remnant survived and retreated deep within the heart of the forest. There, as a coven, they continued their ways, practicing their sorceries and invoking the spirits of their slain progenitors. But over time their bloodline became weak and diluted, and they sought to recreate the Great Incursion, just as it had been in the days of old...the days of the Nephilim.

Hazy struggled against her bonds and winced, her wrists now rubbed raw. The wind howled eerily through the trees as Dargo continued his ponderous monologue.

"And so, fate delivered unto them the man William Darlington. In his preternatural wisdom, he offered up his only daughter to the Coven, to serve as fresh source of blood from which would arise a new breed of Nephilim. They took her and she became with child. But the girl betrayed them and fled, robbing the Coven of their future. Many years later, we found the child. We initiated her bloodletting to open the conduit between worlds...to allow one of the ancient progenitors to pass through and claim her flesh as its own. But the girl had become perverted and twisted by the enemy, and she escaped her fate by the betrayal of one of our own.

For the love of God, just shut up already!

"But out of this misfortune, a chance at redemption has come. For tonight, we will correct the mistakes of the past and honor the oath of William Darlington with a daughter from his bloodline, preserved in secret for generations.

He turned towards Hazy. "Are you ready to receive this great honor?"

She only had one response worth uttering.

"Fuck you."

Dargo chuckled. "Such spirit." he remarked to the Disciples. "That's why she's the perfect choice."

Behind him, Violet glared.

Dargo approached Hazy and bent over to dip his finger in Britney's blood, then smeared the shape of a symbol onto her forehead. Hazy spat in his face. He wiped it away, grinning.

"You truly are my daughter." Dargo turned, extended his arms, and proclaimed into the void, "Tonight we pierce the Veil! We welcome you, ancient powers of old," then reading from the journal, pronounced, "EXTH AETH VEZH OUHM!"

Hazy watched as the darkness before her deepened, becoming thick and impermeable. It wasn't just the absence of illumination. The forest and the ground beneath here seemed to just suddenly…end, as if they stood of the edge of an abyss extending infinitely both ahead and below.

For several moments, silence prevailed. Then, out of the nothingness, the darkness…moved. Tiny pinpricks of light appeared, resolving into the wet gleam of pitch-black eyes. Gray, gaunt limbs appeared, reaching and contorting. Guttural voices breathed blasphemies into her ears as the shadowy void began to close around her. Hazy opened her mouth to scream, but it came out a paralyzed gasp.

A pallid hand reached from the gloom, its long, gnarled fingers tracing the contours of Hazy's body. Then—

Shuk!

—the appendage fell to Hazy's feet with a wet slap against the stone.

An ear-splitting shriek exploded from the dark, followed by a riotous melee.

Hacking.

Splitting.

194

Cracking.

Screeching.

Three words rose above the clamor, uttered in terror and scorn.

"*Shadespawn! Witch Hammer!*"

Hazy strained against her bonds as Dargo slowly backed down off the platform, panic in his eyes. Violet remained in place, transfixed by the unseen horror unfolding before them.

Finally, the yawning chasm spewed forth its foreign intruder like an obscene mockery of childbirth.

The new arrival rose to its feet, dripping with the rancid, black ichor of slain enemies, a brutal, bladed weapon in its grip. Through the gore and viscera, Hazy could discern two piercing blue eyes, fierce and righteous. They looked upon her with recognition and grinned.

Her heart leapt. It was true! It was really true. Nara lived.

The impenetrable dark began to subside like a shadowy mist, revealing two more forms at her sides. Hazy recognized them both. Noel and her brother Simon.

Nara moved quickly, cutting Hazy free. She fell into Nara's arms, and they held each other tight. Hazy wept. "I can't believe it! It's really you!" she cried, wiping away the filth from Nara's face.

Nara smiled. "Thanks to you."

"You have defiled the sanctity of our gathering! Violated our sacred congregation!" Dargo howled, shattering the moment. "Disciples! Show them how we deal with apostates!"

The members the cult reached into their robes and unsheathed sharp, shimmering blades.

"Wait! Wait!" Simon shouted.

Nara spun around.

"I've returned to prove myself to you, father. With an offering." He removed the revolver from behind his back and aimed it at Noel.

Hazy watched Noel's face turn pale as his hands patted around his waist where the gun had been tucked just moments before. He reached for his crossbow, but it was too late.

Simon fired.

Nara screamed.

And Noel collapsed.

CHAPTER 34

Nara cradled Noel's head, one hand pressed hard over the bleeding wound in his chest. She seethed at Simon. "You bastard…"

"An offering?" Dargo asked? "What am I to do with a dying, ex-FBI agent?"

"Not him," Simon clarified. "Her." He motioned towards Nara.

Her blood boiled. She gently released Noel and stood, readying her axe. "You're welcome to try."

Simon kept his focus on Dargo. "I want to trade her for my sister. Let us walk out of here and Nara is all yours."

Dargo smirked. "Are you seeing what I'm seeing, son? By the looks of things, She's the one with the upper hand, not you."

"Really?" He looked Nara in the eye and spoke, "*Muok!*"

Nara's whole body seized as if she had been struck by a bolt of lightning. Her axe dropped from her hand, and she crashed to the dirt, paralyzed. She felt her body turn ice cold, and the edges of her vision darkened.

Hazy rushed to Nara's side and screamed, "Damn it, Simon! What did you do?!"

"I gained her trust. She thought I negated the summoning circle. Instead, I enhanced it, made it a two-way passage. She could travel out, but I allowed something else to travel in. But I kept it trapped behind a layer of wards that could only be released with the right spell. I've just spoken the first half. Let us go, and I will give you the rest. The demon inside of her will be released and take full control. You will have your Nephilim child, ready to begin the line again with fresh blood."

Nara could hear every word, but she was powerless to react. She hated him. She hated herself for letting her guard down. She could feel it…the icy grip of the demon wrenched her very soul, raging to be set free.

"My boy," Dargo said, patting Simon on the back, "I may have been wrong about you. Take your sister. Go."

Hazy glared with red, swollen eyes. "Don't you lay a fucking hand on me!"

She flailed violently as Simon wrapped his arms tight around her and dragged.

"The other half of the spell, Simon," Dargo demanded.

Simon waved his gun back and forth as glowing eyed Disciples began to converge on him.

"You'll get it. Just tell them to back off, Dargo!"

"Stand down, everyone. Let's give the boy a chance. Simon?"

He relented and spoke "*Ahtilat!*"

The demon was loosed, and Nara's world went black.

Hazy didn't waste a second. As soon as Simon spoke, she made her move and delivered a sharp elbow to his stomach. He doubled, dropping the gun. She quickly snatched it up and took aim at Dargo.

He raised his hands, amused. "What's a little girl like you plan to do with a weapon like that?"

"I'll blow your damn brains out. My father...my real father...liked to take his little girl hunting. You're bigger than most things I've taken out."

"Hazy!" Simon screamed "You'll ruin everything! Dargo...father, please! She doesn't know what she's doing. I fulfilled my end of the deal. Let us leave and we'll never bother you again."

"I don't think she wants to leave, Simon. What *do* you want, defiant one?"

"I want to take Nara and get out of here."

Dargo pointed to where Nara lie writhing on the ground. She frothed and spit as the demon began to assert itself.

"You want to take *that* with you? I don't think you realize what you're asking. Why don't you put the gun down and we can discuss a more reasonable solution?"

"No way in Hell."

"Put it down, bitch."

She turned around to witness Violet holding a knife at her brother's throat while two large Disciples restrained him.

Dargo smiled ear to ear. "Oh, this will be fun."

Hazy kept the gun on Dargo, looking back and forth between him and Simon. She could shoot Dargo, then they'd kill her brother. Or she could put the gun down, and then they'd probably kill Simon anyway, and likely her too. Her hand shook as she placed her finger over the trigger.

Nara plummeted through the dark, grasping at anything and everything, desperate to hold on to some small part of herself. The very thing she had pushed against her entire life, the presence that had always malevolently hovered in the shadows, had finally laid claim to its prize. It surrounded her, enveloped her, now *was* her. She could feel the intensity of its gaze and the depravity of its intentions. A voice, both quiet and calamitous, uttered a single word.

"Daughter."

"No!"

"But you know...you've always known. Soultorn. Bloodcursed. Shadespawn. My spawn."

Nara resisted, but she may as well have tried to rescue a single tear drop from the ocean.

"I once walked this Earth. I knew power and conquest. But the Reckoning came, and I was stripped of my flesh, locked behind the Veil, doomed to wander as a restless shade. But my children were faithful. They sought a way back for me. Sara Darlington was bound to me by an oath of blood. By the power of that magic, I transcended my own limitations. I took her and got her with child so that when grown, I might claim its flesh for my own and walk the Earth again. For ordinary man is not sufficient for my strength. I require flesh born of my seed.

"But you were taken from me, and for two hundred years I languished in the Veil...watching, waiting. But today, a wrong has been righted. I am Bolabogg, and I breathe again!"

With her final, fading thoughts, Nara thought of the bravery of her birth mother, the young girl who crossed time and space to deliver her from evil. She called upon her courage, but it wasn't enough.

She thought of the woman who loved her and raised her, who gave her a home and led her to faith. She called upon her strength…those simple words that saved her not once, but twice. *Talitha koum.* "Little girl, arise." But this time, it wasn't enough.

In that moment, Nara knew despair.

Her last thought was of her father.

CHAPTER 35

The air itself seemed to crack and split as the being known as Bolabogg rose to its feet again for the first time in centuries.

Dargo's eyes watered as he fell to his face in reverence. "My lord!" The Disciples followed suit. Simon was released and tossed to the dirt. Violet bowed but kept one eye on Simon and her knife at the ready.

Hazy was the last one to remain standing. She lowered the gun. "Nara?" she questioned, voice quivering.

Bolabogg's eyes glowed green. "Nara Shadespawn, Daughter of Darkness, is no more. Bolabogg lives." The words were deep and resonant.

Hazy broke down, sobbing. "Nara, please!"

"I require the book!"

Dargo arose and approached Bolabogg, handing it the journal. "My lord."

Bolabogg turned and climbed the platform to address the Disciples. Discarded, the axe clanged to the ground. "Recite with me the words in the ancient tongue. For tonight, we reshape the world in my image," the demon declared.

Bolabogg opened the book to the beginning and beheld the fruit of its labor. The girl had dutifully scrawled in blood her own pathetic ramblings with the primeval script it had imparted to her. It was beautiful and perfect. Except…

On the inside front cover…something remained untouched and undefiled. An inscription by another hand. The words, plain and ordinary, were a jolt to the demon's soul.

Her last thought was of her father.

The man who brought her home from the evil dark forest, who guided and protected her, who carried on in love and strength when her mother passed.

The written words, simple and direct, were his.

"Hey, kid. The world is tough. It'll drag you down if you let it. Always remember who you are, where you came from, and that you're always loved. Do that and nothing can stop you. Now get out there and kick some ass. Happy Birthday. Love, Dad."

This time, it was enough.

The being known as Bolabogg fell to its feet for the first time in centuries.

"My lord Bolabogg?" Dargo leapt to his aid but found himself staring into eyes of blue.

"Bolabogg is no more. Nara Kilday lives."

She clutched her axe and with one mighty swing, plunged it deep into Dargo's skull, splitting his head in two.

All hell broke loose as the Disciples began to shout and scatter into the woods—all except the few enhanced by lesser demons. They howled in rage, their eyes glowing bright. There had to be at least a dozen. But Nara was ready for them.

She ran and flew off the platform, landing a death blow to the first before she even hit the ground. She tucked and rolled to avoid the swing from another's blade, then thrust her axe up, severing its arm. She got to her feet, wiped the axe's blade on the bottom of her shoe, and swung for the next one.

Hazy crawled, trying to stay low to avoid the fleeing cultists. She just needed to find a place to hide and take cover. She hoped that the person out there swinging the axe was indeed Nara. She ducked behind one of the crumbling stone mounds, held the revolver close, and prayed she wouldn't need it.

She glanced over to her right and saw someone huddled behind the next mound over. They weren't wearing robes.

"Simon!" she whispered loudly. No response.

She crawled over, calling again. "Simon!"

His head slowly turned in her direction. His face was pale, his eyes lidded. That's when she saw the knife sticking from his chest. In an instant, all of the anger, hatred, and disappointment she felt for him subsided. In that moment, he was just her older brother. The one who took her for ice cream when he first got his license. The one who held her when she cried after their parents fought.

"Simon, damn it," she wept. "What did you do?"

His voice came out faint and raspy. "Violet…"

"Oh, God. Please, Simon. You can't leave me too."

"…messed it all up…so sorry…Nara…"

She buried her head in his neck. "Simon!"

"…tell Dad…"

He breathed his last.

Hazy wept uncontrollably.

Blood gushed like a fountain as Nara pulled her axe from the neck of the last enhanced Disciple. Almost the last. One had hung back, watching...observing. And now it turned to run. Nara took a deep breath, steadied her aim, and launched her axe, clipping him in the shoulder. He fell into the dirt, face first.

Nara marched over and turned him over.

Not him.

Her.

"A—Amanda?!"

Amanda Slater. Her father's new girlfriend. The woman who had moved in on her mother's turf.

Amanda's face contorted in rage. "You fucking whore! You've ruined everything!" she spat.

Her form lurched and shifted, and she struck Nara across the chest with an extended, sinewy arm. Nara flew back, lost her grip on the axe, and collided hard with a column of stones.

Amanda—the thing, whatever it was—discarded its robe and continued to transmogrify until it no longer resembled anything human, rising to nearly eight feet tall. Its eyes were large and black, and its skin clammy and gray. Teeth jutted from its jaw like knives. It reared back and delivered a full body shriek into the night.

Nara's vision swam as she scrambled on all fours, searching for her axe among the brush and hilly mounds of stone. The beast lumbered forward and slammed its foot down on Nara's neck, pinning her to the earth.

"You may have escaped me before, but not today. Your mother begged for her life as I devoured her alive. Let's find out if you are made of sterner stuff. Let's find out if you taste just as sweet."

It was her...Noel had been right. This was the creature he had warned her about. The one who had murdered his family...and her mother.

Nara saw the glint of her axe's blade, wedged between two stones, just out of her reach. The beast bent over and leaned into Nara's face, opening its jaws wide.

Bang!

A shot rang out and found its target in the creature's jaw. Black blood spurted from its mouth as it raised its head to identify the shooter. Hazy stood a few yards away, revolver in hand. She cocked and fired again, this time striking it in the chest. But it seemed to have little effect. The creature howled and launched itself in her direction. She took a deep breath, aimed for the head, and pulled the trigger.

Click.

Click. Click.

Hazy cursed.

The beast lunged...

Thwang.

...and collapsed into a tangle of limbs.

Blood oozed from where the bolt of a crossbow had pierced its throat. Nara rose to her feet to look upon the face of Hazy's savior and breathed a sigh of relief. Noel, covered in sweat, dirt, and blood, leaned against a tree, crossbow in hand. He nodded, and she bent to retrieve her axe.

Nara approached the beast as it writhed and choked on its own blood. It looked up at her with black, soulless eyes and spat. She lifted her axe to deliver the death blow, but it suddenly convulsed, evading her swing. It lurched to its feet and slapped Nara aside like a rag doll, then made a break for the stone platform. It climbed to the top and began waving its hands in precise, fluid motions, bellowing a ragged, guttural chant.

Nara staggered back to her feet, clutching her side where she had been struck. She felt the sharp crackle of air as tendrils of darkness swirled around the beast. It stared back at her with a blackened, malevolent grin and reached for something at its feet. Something red and soiled. It was escaping into the Veil with her journal.

"Nara!" Noel shouted. He was closer, but in his weakened state was struggling to reload to crossbow. It was up to her, and she had one shot. The creature had begun to fade from their reality, completely enveloped by the shadows of the Veil.

Please, God. Nara raised her axe, took aim, and let it fly. It tumbled end over end, slicing through the air and into the dark, swallowed by the void. For a moment, all was silent, and Nara wondered if she had failed. Then a furious shriek split the night as a bloody, dismembered arm dropped out of thin air onto the stone platform with a dull splat. The journal remained clutched in its pale gray hand. The Veil had closed, taking the rest of the creature, and her axe, with it.

Nara fell to her knees, taxed and depleted. The world around her seemed to fade as she yielded to exhaustion. She closed her eyes and felt the warm embrace of her closest friend. For first time in a very long time, she was no longer afraid.

CHAPTER 36

"From chopping heads to turning heads in just under a week. What's your secret?" Hazy asked with a smirk.

She stood with Nara beneath the large banner that hung in the main hall of Darlington High. In bold, blood red letters, it read, "*We Love You, Nara! Welcome Home!*" It seemed every person they passed in the hallways had to stop and say hello or pose for a selfie. The attention turned Nara's stomach.

"Can I just go back to being invisible again?"

"Sorry, Kilday. Your stock has gone way up. Have you not noticed the second looks you're getting from the opposite sex? I say you ride this wave."

"Maybe it's the hair," Nara laughed, flipping her new, shorter locks.

"It's all about the confidence. I'm telling you; people pick up on that stuff. You've changed. And for the better."

"I guess surviving death and taking down a satanic cult does wonders for the self-esteem."

"So, what *did* you tell your dad?"

"Everything."

"Wait? Everything? The dying? Resurrection? The monsters?"

"Okay, maybe not everything."

"But you said he said saw you basically beam out of the basement of Pitch Black."

"I thought he did. He hasn't really brought it up. But that's my dad. He's knows a lot of stuff but plays it close to the vest. Plays aloof. Comes with being a cop, I guess. I have a pretty good sense he knows a lot more about what happened, but he's too cool to let on."

"Hey, Nara!" Duane Rodd called out as he raced down the hall on his way to football practice.

Nara and Hazy turned to each other and burst out laughing.

"See? What did I tell you?"

Nara rolled her eyes. "So anyway, your dad still doing better?"

"Like, a thousand percent. I don't get it Nara, I really don't. It's like, as soon as all of this was over, he sprang back. Do you think maybe…"

"What?"

Hazy lowered her voice. "I know this sounds crazy, but that maybe it was the cult? That they did something to him?"

"Simon told me…" Nara hesitated, careful to avoid salting wounds that had yet to heal. "He said everything he did was for his family. I wouldn't be at all surprised if they kept your dad sick as a way to control Simon."

Hazy stopped and looked around, making sure no one was too close to hear. "Do you think what Dargo said was true?" she asked, eyes downcast, her voice barely above a whisper. That he…that Simon and I…?"

"I don't know," Nara replied, pushing back against the specter of her own dark lineage. "Your father is the man who loved and raised you. If you ask me, that's all that really matters in the end."

After all they'd been through over the years, it turned out that she and Hazy had been bound by something more than simple friendship. Nara wondered—was that what had drawn them together? The hand of fate or the machinations of unseen force?

They resumed their walk, oblivious to the constant stares and whispers from passers-by. "It's just so crazy to think that William Darlington…going back far enough, is our grandpa. What would that make us? Like…cousins or something?" Hazy mused.

Nara chuckled. "Something like that. Pretty wild, huh?"

Hazy's eyes suddenly grew wide. "Speaking of wild, check this out!" They had arrived at Nara's locker, completely decked out in decorations, notes, and flowers.

"I'm never going to get used to this." As she leaned inside to retrieve her Algebra book, Hazy caught a glint of silver tucked under Nara's shirt.

"You know I won't be offended if don't want to wear that anymore, right? With all that's happened, I think I can appreciate a little aversion to anything remotely linked to the dark side."

Nara reached into her shirt to pull out the pentagram necklace, modified so that the star now hung inverted. "When you gave it to me, you said something about giving it my own meaning." She held it in her palm, running her thumb along the crack that split it down the center. "I think I have."

Nara shut her locker door. "Besides, it led me back to you."

Hazy smiled, but Nara perceived that it was bittersweet. "Okay, gotta go. Tonight?"

"I'll be there," Nara said, as she watched her disappear down the bustling hallway. She looked back at the large "Welcome Home" banner and the decorations hanging on her locker. She knew it was all temporary, that the town had just needed their moment to celebrate *something* positive after all the misery of the past few months. The truth was that three girls were dead and never going home to their families. Violet was missing, and as far as everyone in the town knew, so was Hans Dargo. The Disciples had disposed of his body along with the rest of the members Nara had slain. Mainstream acceptance of the cult's existence had gained momentum, but Nara knew most people would relegate it all to the realm of rumors and conspiracies, despite her claims to the contrary. The Disciples would continue to live among them, hiding in plain sight, plotting, and planning. But Nara would be watching and ready.

◣⊱⊰◢

"Hey! How's my favorite living dead girl?" Noel shouted as Nara stepped into his hospital room.

Nara's eyes grew big as saucers. "Noel! Shhh!"

"Oh, sorry," he said, lowering his voice to a whisper. "Must be all the drugs."

"You sound like you're feeling better."

"Yeah, great. Just ready to get out of here. How about you?"

"I'm good. Pretty good."

"That doesn't sound convincing."

"All the attention is weird. And I'm not crazy about having to keep up a cover story for what really happened to me. But mostly…" She sat down in the chair at his bedside. "…I guess I just don't know where I'm supposed to go from here. I mean what if…*it* comes back? What if it never actually left? What if it's still inside me, just waiting to take control again?"

"I don't believe that. Nara, you went up against a six-thousand-year-old demon and won. You've shown who you really are. It's what's in here that matters," he said, pointing towards her heart. "Not where you came from."

"Thanks, I guess."

"Hey, you two!" Nara's dad announced as he entered the room, beaming.

"Hey, Dad!" she exclaimed as she leapt up to hug him.

"I just wanted to come by and let Mister Raddemer know that he's officially been cleared as a suspect. I'm going to do everything I can to make sure everyone knows you're the hero of this story. You brought my daughter home…twice now," he added. "I owe you."

"That's not really necessary, Sheriff. The way I see it, I was just returning the favor. You fulfilled a promise I wasn't able to keep," Noel said, looking at Nara. "And did a better job of it than I ever could have."

"Well, her mother did all the hard work. All I had to do was not screw it up. Which reminds me. Nara, when you're done here, can you meet me down in the parking lot?"

"Yeah, sure. Okay."

"All right. I'll leave you to it. Feel better, Mister Raddemer," her dad said with a parting wave.

Nara turned back to Noel and shrugged her shoulders. "So. Once you get out of here, what's next? Back to the FBI?"

"Hell, no. Never again. I've had plenty of time to think, though. And I've decided I'm going to rebuild that church in the woods. The Church of the Protectorate. But do it all proper this time. What do you think?"

"Wow. That sounds…"

"Crazy? Yeah. But the evil out there…it didn't just go away. It's been there a very long time and it's patient. We need a watchman. Someone out there on the front lines so nothing like this sneaks up on us again. But not just me. Others too. People of like minds. Maybe even you."

"I don't know. I've already got a church—"

"This isn't that kind of church. I mean it is, but it isn't." Noel leaned forward and lowered his voice. "I'm talking about a fully armed outpost ready to take on anything that comes crawling out of those God forsaken woods. The thing that killed my family…your birth mother? It's still out there. And more just like it. What happened to us…I'll never let it happen to anyone again."

"That sounds more like a militia than a church."

"Maybe it is. But are you in?"

The elevator dinged, and out stepped Elijah. He didn't look up and nearly collided with Nara.

"Elijah, hey!"

"Oh, hey. Sorry. Didn't see you there." He continued walking, head held low.

"Hey, wait a minute. How's your dad?"

He stopped. "They're releasing him today. I'm actually here to pick him up. So…"

"That's great."

He turned to keep walking.

"Are you avoiding me? I haven't heard from you at all since I've been back. I've tried texting, calling…"

He kept his head down, avoiding eye contact. "I've just been trying to let you have your space."

"I've had plenty of space, believe me. I want to be with my friends again. Everything that happened…that's all in the past now. I hope we can move forward, you know? Start again?"

"I don't know. I don't think I'm ready for anything like that."

"Oh. Okay," she replied, taken aback.

"I gotta go."

She watched him go with the sobering realization that the hardest part of all of this was the fact that there was no going back to the way things used to be. Not ever.

Nara stepped out of the main entrance of St. Joan's Hospital and scanned the parking lot. She didn't see her dad anywhere. She dialed him on her phone. "Where are you?"

"Straight ahead. See me waving? I'm in the silver hatchback."

Wait. What?

She jogged to the car, where her father waited inside— in the passenger seat. She opened the driver's side door.

"Can I get a lift?" he asked with big grin.

"What is this?" She asked, stunned. "Is this…? No!"

"Happy birthday!"

She jumped inside and wrapped her arms around his neck, bursting with tears.

"Oh, my God! Thank you, thank you, thank you!"

"Hey, hey! She's nothing special. Got a few miles on her, probably needs a new transmission. But she'll get you where you need to go."

"No, Dad. This is amazing. Thank you. You're the best!"

"Nah. Just figured I really owed you after...you know."

"Dad, you don't owe me anything. You've given me more than you'll ever know."

"Well, what are you waiting for? Start her up!"

She turned the ignition. The sound of the engine starting up was music to her ears. She clapped ecstatically. "I can't believe this is mine!"

"How about that birthday dinner, huh? Just you and me?"

An image of Amanda mutating into a witch demon flashed in her mind.

"I wasn't too crazy about Amanda, but I'm sorry she just ghosted you like that. That wasn't cool." She had a tinge of guilt about not totally coming clean with him, but what was she supposed to say? *Your girlfriend escaped into another dimension after she tried to eat my face?*

"It's okay," he said. "I think I was ready for it to be done anyway."

"Oh. I thought that, you know...while I was gone that you two might have gotten closer."

"Pretty much the opposite, actually. As it went on, it became clear to me that the sweet church lady routine was just an act. She wasn't the real deal. Not like your mom."

"Not many people are."

"That's the truth. She was a special lady. She'd be so proud of the young woman you've turned out to be." He turned his head away from her and stared out the window. Nara reached for his hand.

He turned back, smiling through watering eyes.

"So? Norma's? I got a hankering for some cherry pie."

"Norma's it is."

Nara put the car into gear, performed her first successful reverse, and exited the parking lot onto Main.

ハ.ジム·

"I never thought I'd be back here so soon," Nara said.

It was a beautiful night with a clear sky and a full moon. The stars shone bright.

"Thank you for coming," Hazy said. "I know it's not easy. But it means a lot to me."

They stood within the circle of standing stones, now cracked and beginning to crumble. Hazy lit a candle on the remains of the altar and picked up the urn.

"He loved it out there. These woods, with all their mysteries and secrets. It led him to a bad place, but I don't think there's anywhere else he'd rather be."

She opened the urn and turned it over, letting his ashes scatter in the breeze.

"I love you, Simon." She broke down and sobbed. Nara held her close, and for a long time they just stared up into the night sky, Hazy's head on her shoulder.

Hazy broke the long silence. "Mom said she wants to stay and try to work things out with Dad."

"No kidding? How do you feel about that?"

"I don't know. Good, but sad. I hate that this is what it took to bring them back together."

"Maybe, in a way, it's Simon's parting gift to you. If nothing else, he really cared about you. He fought for you 'til the bitter end."

"Only one thing I know for sure: if Violet ever shows her face around here again, I'll fucking kill her." She stood up, brushed off her jeans, and adjusted her headband. "Okay, a deal's a deal. You still want to go through with it?"

"I think so."

"You think so? You sounded a lot more sure earlier."

"That's why I need your help. I don't trust myself to go through with it alone."

Hazy reached inside her duffel bag for the metal bucket and lighter fluid Nara had asked her to pack. "Do you have it?"

Nara removed the journal from her backpack. She caressed its cover, already beginning to second guess herself.

"You can do this." Hazy said. Remember what you told me. If the cult gets its hands on it again, there's no telling what they might be able to accomplish."

Nara opened the journal to the final entry she had written earlier that day.

"Shadespawn, they call me, reborn under a midnight moon.

Devils cursed and darkness fled as I rose from my shallow tomb

Through time and space
and cursed earth

A mother's love redeemed my birth

Now Death has failed to claim its prize

Sin's debt is paid. Little girl, arise

I've seen beyond the Veil.

Hell will not prevail."

Nara closed the book and took one last longing look at it before placing it into the bucket.

"I hope I don't regret this," Nara said somberly. "Do it."

Hazy doused the journal with lighter fluid then handed a match to Nara. "You want to do the honors?"

Nara struck the match and dropped it into the bucket. The journal ignited in a *whoosh* of flames.

They placed the bucket within the shattered remains of the altar and walked away hand in hand, leaving the journal to burn. They passed out of the circle and began their hike out of the woods in silence, until a glint in the dark caught Hazy's eye. "What's that?"

As they approached the object, Nara gasped. "No way!" She dug through the brush to retrieve it, gripping its solid form with both hand, it's blade gleaming.

Hazy observed quizzically. "I don't get it. Didn't your axe disappear into the Veil with that monster?"

"Yes. And No. It's complicated. I can't exactly say I get it either."

The handle grew suddenly hot in her hands, and she watched as three familiar symbols formed on its surface, as if being etched by an unseen hand.

"But I think we're going to find out."

vı.☾⚅.

In the early morning hours, just before the break of dawn, a cloaked figure stepped into the circle. She removed her hood, letting her raven locks flutter in the soft, cool breeze. She reached into the bucket and retrieved the journal, slightly charred and smoking, but mostly intact. The girl smiled. She knew it would take more than mere fire to destroy it. She continued her walk into the woods, taking the book with her.

She came to it at last, the stone pedestal where the Veil between worlds had been breached. She climbed to the top and removed her robe, her pale, naked skin practically glowing in the light of the moon. She lifted her dagger, kissed its blade, then slashed it across her palm. She opened the journal, studied it, then used her blood to paint symbols of invitation, submission, and consummation onto her body.

She stood to face the deep of the woods, lifted her arms, and loudly proclaimed, "I, Violet Grey, daughter of Hans Dargo, invoke my right as descendant of William Darlington, to fulfill his oath and offer myself to the dweller in the Veil."

She laid down upon the cold stone, eyes closed, and awaited a response.

The demon answered.

ACKNOWLEDGMENTS

Special thanks to Jack Heller for his encouragement, support, and belief in *Dead@17*, and to Brendan Deneen for graciously showing me the ropes and finding the right home for this book. It would not exist without either of you.

My gratitude to Heather King and my editors, Mal Windsor and Anika Claire, at Permuted Press for their invaluable guidance and contributions towards making *Dead@17* the best it can be.

ABOUT THE AUTHOR

Josh Howard is an accomplished writer and artist, having created numerous comics, graphic novels, and illustrations for Sony, Mattel, DC Comics, Image Comics, and more. *Dead@17* is his first novel.

Photo credit: Laura Howard